Denton Welch was born on 29 March 1915 in Shanghai, where his father was a businessman. He was the youngest of three brothers and particularly close to his American mother, an enthusiastic Christian Scientist who was to die when he was eleven. Welch was sent back to England to attend St Michael's prep school in Uckfield, and then Repton School, where his main achievements were in art. Soon after his sixteenth birthday he ran away from school, an episode later described in his first autobiographical book, *Maiden Voyage* (Routledge, 1943). With his family's approval he enrolled at the Goldsmiths' School of Art in April 1933 to study painting. He showed great promise as an artist but in June 1935, while still a student, he was knocked off his bicycle by a motorist, severely damaging his spine and kidneys; for the rest of his life he was a semi-invalid. The accident and his long convalescence, minutely detailed, form the basis of *A Voice Through a Cloud*, which was unfinished at his death. It was first published in 1950 by John Lehmann and reissued in 2004 by Enitharmon Press.

Welch settled in Kent, in a succession of rented flats and cottages. His final home was Middle Orchard in the village of Crouch, where his faithful friend Eric Oliver – eventually his literary executor – cared for him until his premature death on 30 December 1948. In the last five years of his life Welch received much encouragement from other writers, notably Edith Sitwell, E. M. Forster and Herbert Read, and the majority of his work dates from this period. After *Maiden Voyage* was given enthusiastic reviews, his reputation as a writer increased rapidly and was further enhanced by *In Youth Is Pleasure* (Routledge, 1945; Enitharmon Press, 2005). His remaining stories were published in *Brave and Cruel* (Hamish Hamilton, 1949) and *A Last Sheaf* (John Lehmann, 1951), which also included poems and reproductions of paintings. Other posthumous publications were a collection of poems, *Dumb Instrument* (Enitharmon Press, 1976), and *The Journals of Denton Welch*, edited by Michael De-la-Noy (Allison & Busby, 1984; Penguin, 1987). The main biographies have been Michael De-la-Noy's *Denton Welch: the Making of a Writer* (Viking, 1984) and James Methuen-Campbell's *Denton Welch: Writer and Artist* (Tartarus Press, 2002).

DENTON WELCH

I Left My Grandfather's House

ENITHARMON

Published in 2006
by Enitharmon Press
26B Caversham Road
London NW5 2DU

www.enitharmon.co.uk

First published in a limited edition by
The Lion & Unicorn Press at the RCA, 1958

Distributed in the UK by
Central Books
99 Wallis Road
London E9 5LN

ISBN 1 904634 28 1 (hardback)

Enitharmon Press gratefully acknowledges the financial support of
Arts Council England, London.

British Library Cataloguing-in-Publication Data.
A catalogue record for this book is available
from the British Library.

The frontispiece and the watercolour on page 87 are by Denton Welch,
from the collection of Richard Hutchings.

Typeset in Bembo by Servis Filmsetting Ltd
and printed in England by Cromwell Press

In the early summer of 1933 I started out for my first walking tour. I left my grandfather's house at Henfield in Sussex one evening and walked towards the river. My aunt seemed pleased to be rid of me. She speeded me on my way rather too gaily and quickly.

As I walked, I thought, 'I've really started now, and I don't know where I am going to sleep tonight.' I felt excited, but also a little unhappy and alarmed. I wished that I had not started out in the evening.

I had been planning my tour all the weeks that I had walked to and from the art school in the squalid London streets. I thought, 'I shall get away from all this and wear only a shirt and shorts and not go near anyone for weeks and weeks.' I had a longing to hide myself in some very isolated place, and I thought immediately of the Lakes. I wanted to go to them; I had never seen them, but I can't remember what made me finally change my plans and walk to Devonshire instead. It may have been that I knew the way, roughly, in that direction, or it may have been because there were more hostels in the south and west. I had decided to stay in Youth Hostels whenever I could.

When I got to the river banks the sun still seemed high but it was turning orange. I spoke to an old man who was smoking his pipe near the water and asked him if it was Steyning that I could see on the other bank. He said it was and added something that I cannot remember, but I know that it gave me a dismal feeling, a realization that I was alone, that it was getting late and I had nowhere to sleep.

I came out into the town by the church. I remembered the day when I had drawn one of its Norman arches, and this too, for some reason, added to my gloom. I hurried past the old school and on into the High Street. I saw again what my aunt had said was the mint-house. I thought of coins and counterfeiters. The Georgian front of the hotel and all the other houses made me feel sad. I felt that they were all threatened, that nothing could survive for long. I passed the tea-shop (near the old building with the cupola), where my aunt always bought cakes and soda-bread; I thought of the thick chocolate icing and the walnuts. I almost longed to be back at Whaphams helping to stir the coffee in the machine after supper.

When I reached the end of the town and was on the road to Washington I spoke to another man. I asked him if he knew where I could spend the night. He seemed doubtful; he thought I might find something if I went down the lane to Wiston. He thought that there was a cottage at the end, on the left, where they might take me in.

I turned into the lane, past the old beamed house with the jutting out upper storeys on each side. The light was beginning to fade; a rich blue mist was smeared and wrapped round things. When I got to the cottage I did not dare to ask; I went to the front door, then to the back, and finally left without saying anything. I shut the garden gate as quietly as possible and walked on in the direction of Wiston, feeling a little desperate.

I had seen the great house before, but only in the full daytime and never when I was alone. Now it looked majestic as ever, with all its Elizabethan stonework, but there was something baleful and forbidding about it too. I think that some panes must have been glittering in the last light or that some lurid colour must have caught its chimneys. I know it filled me with disquiet.

I walked up to the courtyard in front and stared at its sulking face. Suddenly its ancientness delighted me. I loved the eighteenth-century sash window stuck carelessly in the Elizabethan stonework. I loved all its crude ornaments. I had the idea from my aunt that the Gorings, who owned it, had let it. I thought that it might be empty and that a good-natured housekeeper might give me a servant's bedroom when I told her how far I had walked.

Without allowing myself to think too much I strode up to the jutting-out porch and pulled the long iron handbell. The noise, echoing a long way off, frightened me. I was confusing myself with explanations as the footsteps approached. 'Who'll it be?' I thought, and, 'What shall I say?'

The door opened slowly and a young footman in striped waistcoat and carrying an electric torch stood in front of me. He had dark eyes and dark hair and he stared at me in some surprise.

'I wonder if you could tell me of anywhere where I could spend the night,' I said hurriedly. 'I'm on a walking tour, and I haven't found anywhere yet, although I was told of a cottage out in this direction.' All the time I was willing him to say that he'd go and ask if I could spend the night there.

But he only looked at me quite pleasantly and stupidly and said, 'There's nothing out here, I'm afraid. You'll have to go back to Steyning.'

'Oh, I can't do that, I've walked too far, I'm very tired,' I answered.

The man thought for a moment or two.

'I suppose it wouldn't be possible for me to put up in some odd corner here, just for the night?' I suggested in a rush of boldness.

'No, I don't think you could do that,' he said heavily. 'I'd get into trouble, but I was going to say why not go round to the farm and ask if you can sleep in one of the outhouses? One of them's got plenty of clean hay in it.'

The suggestion seemed somehow insulting, but I knew it was sensible. I said good-night and turned away, feeling affronted that I should have to ask for room in an outhouse and not in the great house.

I found the small farm down the lane, and knocked. The farmer looked suspicious and worn-down, as less prosperous ones usually do. I told him what the footman had suggested to me and he took me to the shed. The entire floor was thickly covered in hay, so that the little room seemed like some enormous old box-bed.

I thanked him and he left me after saying a few rather tense, discontented things. I sat down in the hay and started to unpack my rucksack. I could not clean my teeth without water, so I contented myself with rubbing toothpaste along the ridges of my teeth. I realized now how tired I was. I felt two blisters on my heels. I rubbed them with Vaseline, hoping that it might do some good; then I loosened my belt, wrapped myself in my mackintosh and burrowed into the hay. I felt uncomfortable and rather miserable. The hay pricked my face and irritated. 'I'm really sleeping out, the first time in my life!' I thought. I felt that the night was going to be very long and dreary.

Someone was standing in the doorway of the shed. I could see his silhouette against what light remained. He came up to me, shone a torch and said, 'Hullo'. He told me that he was the farmer's son and that he was sixteen. I told him that I was eighteen and that I was going to walk to Devonshire. He began to ask me a lot of questions about what I did and whether I slept out every night. It embarrassed me a little to talk about art school but I told him about it, because it seemed to interest and impress him. I told him that I'd never slept out before and suggested, jokingly, that he should come out and join me in the hay as I was afraid of ghosts. He was shining the torch up in the air now and I could see his face in the dim light. It was a nice face – rather blunt and strong with a broad nose. He was seriously considering the suggestion; it was an adventure, and he wanted to be nice to me. But at last he said, 'I'd better not; my old man wouldn't like it. I'll stay out here and talk to you a bit though.'

I was torn between wanting to sleep and not wanting to be left alone. I let him ask his questions and teased him a little by making startling remarks and joking with him. I remember him now as a person who was just emerging from his chrysalis; he seemed a little timid, but ready to try everything for himself.

He said good-night and got up to go.

'Perhaps I'll see you in the morning,' I said.

'Perhaps. Have a good night. Don't let the fleas bite.'

He was nice; I liked him.

The night gradually wore away. I was constantly pricked and irritated by the hay. I began to hate it, but it kept me warm. I had troubled dreams about disgusting people, smelling of sweat, and with black, broken finger-nails.

The last time I woke up I saw that it was already light. It was, I think, about a quarter past four. I decided to get up and walk to the top of the Downs, to see the sun rise from Chanctonbury Ring, the Ancient British earthwork, which some eighteenth-century Goring had planted with a ring of trees.

I packed my rucksack, fluffed out the hay and then started to walk up the lane. I decided that it was too early to make any call at the farmhouse. I felt slightly sick and my blisters hurt, but the morning was promising to be wonderful. A thick dew was spread over every-thing and the number of heavy-laden spangled cobwebs in the ditches fascinated me.

The lane became a path through a field. As I came up to a log of wood I gave a start, for there, lying beside the log, was a creature dressed all in rags so that he looked like a tattered, scaling tree trunk. I looked down on him with a certain amount of horror and fear; I thought he might be dead. When I knew that he was only sleeping I looked at all the details of his appearance. He was old, with a wicked, outcast's face, and his decayed trilby had been fantastically remodelled into a sort of cone. His head was supported on the rest of his possessions and he lay on his back with his hands and legs thrown out carelessly.

After one last fascinated look I walked on hurriedly. I did not want to wake him. I saw clearly the accumulated horror of waking for such a person. Also, I thought he might threaten me, or beg. 'To think that he's been there, so close, all through the night!' I said. 'He might have murdered me or stolen all my things.'

I began to climb, past the chalk pit, past the tangle of trees and the first dew pond. I thought of our picnics here as schoolboys, when my brother Paul and Basil Ball from Dartmouth had raced about like mad things.

The steepness of the last part was painful. I caught hold of twigs and trees to pull myself up. At last I stood on the edge of the ring. The trees were soughing mournfully. I looked out across what seemed like all Sussex, and waited. Gradually all the heavy grey was lightened and transmuted into gold. It really was gold, for there was a glint and a flash about everything. I stood looking at it, thinking that I ought to be more impressed by such a wonder. I knew it was wonderful but I could feel very little, except that my teeth were chattering and that I felt sick and empty and lonely.

I went to look through the trees at the heart of the earthwork, then I started out along the other crest of the hill, determining to walk a long way and then dip down for breakfast.

My teeth were still chattering violently. I felt that I should never get warm. In the distance, as I walked along the huge grey hummock of the Downs, I saw what looked like a cottage. I wondered what it could be, so small and so isolated on the windy ridge.

It *was* a cottage, or rather, the remnant of one. Even at some distance it looked deserted. I could see the broken windows and blackened paintwork. On one side, broken-down walls framed what once had been a garden or small farmyard.

I climbed over one of the gaps and let myself into the cottage. There was still a door to one of the openings; the place where the handle had been was black and smooth and greasy from many hands. The main room had the same disgusting quality about it; the wall-paper was brown with filth and smoke, some of it hung in tatters, and a fungus grew in one corner. I was surprised to see a table in the middle of the room and on it opened tins, a blue sugar bag and cigarette stubs. There were fish bones on the floor, and excrement. Over the mantelpiece someone had scrawled an obscene couplet, in chalk found on the Downs, I supposed. I could not quite make the words out and stood staring at them for some moments; then I was overcome with horror and dislike of the place. I thought of the tramps and vagabonds stopping at the derelict house for one night of their never ending journey. I thought of it when the wind screamed through the sacking nailed over the windows, and when the rotting beams creaked. One day it would all come down, I thought. It would give a sickening lurch and be flat, and I wondered if any tramps would be buried under it.

I climbed through the hole in the wall again and ran away from the cottage at top speed. I had decided to dip down to see Amberly and to buy food for my breakfast there.

Although I had been walking for hours, it was still very early. The morning mist was just beginning to melt as I entered the village. Dew sparkled on the coarse broad leaves in the ditch, and the garden walls seemed crumbling and soft. I walked between the thatched cottages and thought it the most untouched village I had yet seen. Nothing had been painted garish black and white, or given a false look. There was a sort of greenish messy patina over the thatch, the tiles and the creamy walls. I supposed that cars did go down the uneven streets, but at this early hour everything was still. It seemed very much like a village sleeping under a spell.

I found a shop at last, just opened, and bought biscuits, cheese, butter, jam, a tin of cream and tomatoes. With the food in my ruck-sack I began to feel extremely hungry. I hurried down a street which led to what looked like the ruins of a castle. I decided to picnic at the foot of the ruins. I thought I would try to explore the church, which was nearby, and the castle, after my meal. A little path led down under the huge wall to the fields where a small stream flowed. I sat down by the stream and started to spread out my food on a corner of my raincoat. I found my tin-opener and opened the cream in readiness; then I began to eat the biscuits and butter and cheese and tomatoes greedily, and after that the biscuits and jam and cream. The rich cream had the sickly tinned flavour but I found it delicious at first.

I lay back on the grass, full and satisfied; then I washed my knife and plate in the stream and got up. I started to walk along the foot of the wall where the cattle had been. It seemed to lead to nowhere, so I retraced my steps and climbed up to the church. I can remember nothing about it except some flower-beds, a notice board, and two old ladies talking at the gate.

I went up to a gate in the farther wall and read that I could look over the castle ruins if I paid a shilling. So I went in and saw that a newish house had been built among the ruins. The outer wall of the castle surrounded it and enclosed the garden on every side except one. I walked round, looking at the fireplaces marooned high up in the walls and at the grim-looking little arches and closets. No one came to claim my shilling, so I walked back into the churchyard. The old ladies were still there.

I set out on my way again, crossing the Arun in a ferry-boat, which seemed medieval and charming enough to me. The sun was shining brilliantly now, and I climbed up to Bury joyfully and looked at the church there. It seemed like a chapel, and I thought it was not old, until I realized that this effect was created by the fact that the whole building was Early English with slender lancet windows. I went in but there was an air of depression about it. I seem to remember grim wooden blocks of unpolished parquet floor, and a baize curtain stamped with fleurs-de-lis and held up by a tarnished brass-lacquered rod.

I went away, thinking how I would like to restore the church. I began to climb up again on to the Downs. At one point some large trees were being cut down. A very fine young man was working in one corner of the wood. I watched his axe swing several times, then ventured a few words; but he did not seem to want to talk. He took a swig from his bottle, wiped his hand across his sweating face, then went in search of another woodman.

I picked some berries off a bush and moved on. I was beginning to feel lonely. All that afternoon I walked with too much grim determination. Towards tea-time I dipped down again and came out by a group of cottages which looked as if they had been built as alms-houses or homes for the labourers on a big estate.

Two women stood in the hot, dusty, white road in front of the houses. They looked at me as I passed but said nothing. A few moments later one of them caught me up. She was plump and carried a basket.

'You must be tired; wouldn't you like a cup of tea?' she said sweetly.

I was very surprised.

'Thank you very much,' I said. 'I am rather tired. I've been walking a long way.'

'I live just up here,' she said, leading me to one of the cottages.

Inside it was very full, but very neat, if stuffy. There was an oleograph of a terrier tearing up a poor child's rag doll and several photographs of stolid men in uniform. The woman took the kettle, which was already on the range, and soon had it boiling. She poured the water into the brown teapot with the red-rubber spout, and cut some thick slices of bread which she buttered. She handed me a large white cup with a piece of bread and butter in the saucer. I thanked her and she smiled contentedly.

'This is your lucky day,' she said. She seemed to be almost crooning to herself with pleasure.

I said again what a pleasant surprise it was to have so much kindness. I could see how much her action meant to her. She tapped the table dreamily and repeated, 'This'll be one of your lucky days.' There was a pause. 'My husband will be in any moment now,' she added. 'He'll be pleased I asked you in, too.'

I got up to go, not wanting to thank the husband as well as the wife. I told her again how grateful I was, and she accepted it all. She saw me to the door and smiled hazily all over her face as she wished me luck on my journey and asked God to bless me.

I trudged on down the white road, thinking of the woman and wondering where I should spend the night.

A few miles on I came to a tiny hamlet; there only seemed to be a pub and a few cottages. I went into the pub and asked if they had a room for me. There was talk and argument behind the bar and then a girl took me up to a bare little room with coarse lace curtains. I was so tired that anything would have looked delightful to me. I said I would have it, but even as I spoke the lady of the house climbed up the stairs, painfully calling out between her gasps for breath that she was very sorry she couldn't manage to have anybody, as the girl went home in the evenings and she had no one to help with the meals.

I said that I could eat what I had with me and that all I needed was a bed. I told them that I had already walked over thirty miles that day and that I could go no further. The thought of being turned out made me feel desperate, but the landlord's wife only looked at me sorrowfully and said again with firmness, 'I'm sorry, I couldn't manage it.'

I was so angry that I regained some energy. I pushed down the stairs, shouting over my shoulder what I thought of her. She was still wheezing and gasping a sort of apology as I jerked open the door and let myself out.

I was determined to get to Midhurst somehow; I knew that I would get no shelter anywhere else. But the thought of the four or five miles to that town so appalled me that I often despaired of reaching it. I asked everyone I passed how far it was and their different answers maddened me.

'It can't be so far as that,' I rapped out to one old man who told me it was six miles.

'You seem to know more'n I do,' he drawled laconically; then turned his back and left me staring down the road.

I walked on, noticing hardly anything except that the light was turning to red and gold. A tawny haystack, its neatly cut sections lit up into flaming steps by the evening glow, sticks in my mind, and the black threads of the telephone wires against the higher, bird's-egg-blue sky. The colour was so thin and pure that it sent one weak dart of pleasure through all my tiredness.

I came into the town in a sort of daze. I felt that I could never stop walking, for if I did I would lie where I fell for ever. I saw the Spread Eagle before me. It looked so welcoming that I could have cried. I climbed up the steps and spoke to the girl in the office.

'Have you a single room for the night?' I asked firmly, becoming acutely conscious of the sweat on my face, the mud on my shoes and my shorts and open shirt.

The correct demure-looking girl gave me rather an amused but quite friendly look.

'Ought I to bring out my money and offer to pay now, or does a rucksack "count" as luggage?' I asked myself. Then I decided that I would make no concessions, that they must take me as I was and be pleased to do it. I bolstered myself up with a little arrogance.

'Yes, sir,' the girl said, in a tone of voice which seemed to show that she thought she was good-naturedly playing an amusing part.

'We've got a single room; I'll show you up to it.' She looked at me more closely. 'You must be tired, but it's been a lovely day.'

She led me down a long passage, which seemed very low and broad; there was a rich red carpet on the floor, which troubled my eyes as I looked down at it. She left me at the door of the neat little room, which had 'hotel' written all over it, from the notices about meals, tipping and the lights, down to the green waste-paper basket sprayed with gold paint.

I shut the door behind her and latched it; then I cleaned my teeth, washed my face and hands and remembered that I had packed no pyjamas. I got into bed in my cotton shirt and lay there, not able to go to sleep for some time. This is what being 'over-tired' means, I thought. I never used to believe that you could be too tired to go to sleep; now I do.

I was still walking in my dreams for most of the night. When the maid knocked on my door in the morning, I remembered it was latched. I wondered if I could jump out of bed, open the door, and jump in again before she could see that I only wore a shirt. I decided to risk it, and darted my naked legs and thighs under the bed clothes just as she brought in the tea.

She was plump and round, rather waxy and Dutch-dollish with her wide unsmart maid's cap. She looked at my rucksack and asked me if I'd walked very far the day before and whether I felt rested.

As she spoke I realized that my body ached and that my back and legs were stiff; but it did not feel unpleasant, it seemed rather delicious. I told her modestly that I had walked more than thirty-five miles the day before; and I took pleasure when I saw her mouth gape open in astonishment.

She left me and I drank the tea contentedly. I opened *Wuthering Heights* which I had brought with me, but I felt again that it is a pity and a waste to read a book for pure pleasure, more than once. Read it to study it, read it to know it, but do not read it only for delight again, I thought.

I bathed and shaved and came back to pack up my rucksack. I put in my washing things, my ivory comb, *Wuthering Heights*, but must have forgotten the George IV spoon with the Prince of Wales feathers on it, which I had found amongst the greasy base-metal cutlery at school, and which I had appropriated to myself with such satisfaction, two years before. I had often wondered how it came to be mixed with the modern stuff, and if it had originally belonged to an inn called the Prince of Wales.

I suppose the maid found it on the washstand after I had left and took it down to the kitchen. I did not miss it until that night, when it was too late to go back.

I went down to the dining-room and ate the whole large hotel breakfast: grapefruit, porridge (with that special hotel castor sugar), eggs, toast, marmalade and coffee. I wished that the other guests had not looked quite so respectable and bourgeois. Their ties, tweed coats and imitation pearls made my bare knees and throat feel specially naked.

I paid my bill. The girl of the night before was not there. Then I walked down the steps into the sun, wishing that hotels were less expensive or that I had more money. I was sorry to leave the fifteen-odd shillings on the desk.

I walked down the street to where two swans were sailing on a rather murky pond. As I leant over the railings the two birds began to make love, or rather the male bird became masterful and vicious, and tried to bend the other to his will. I watched them fascinated, but also a little ashamed of what passers-by might think of this spectacle and my close attention to it. There was much flapping of huge oily wings and splashing of water as the male chased the female and pinned her down at last. The wicked swan necks turned and darted and the flat beaks snapped. The heavy bodies sank lower in the brown water. I turned away and asked someone where Cowdray was. I wanted to see the ruins.

It looked almost inhabitable as I first came upon it. I walked under the gateway and bought a little booklet on the house. I read of Dr Johnson's visit, of the curse on the family – that it should perish by fire and water.

Across the court, in the great hall, a group of others were staring up at the walls. I passed them and went into the chapel where pieces of eighteenth-century-looking plasterwork still clung to the arches of the windows. I climbed up to what was marked on my little map as Queen Elizabeth's room. The fireplace had been bricked up and made smaller at several different times. I took note of this for some reason.

I thought of the house on the night of the fire, when the young owner was in Germany, soon to be drowned. I imagined the house-keeper, running from room to room, half-mad with despair.

Standing in what once had been a window in Queen Elizabeth's room, I looked across the light golden cornfields and wished again that I had someone to talk to. 'Perhaps I will find someone,' I thought, 'as I walk along today.' I tried to throw off my depression and went to look at the huge octagonal kitchen, the only roofed-in part.

I thought with delight of the whole ruin as belonging to me. I would live in the wonderful kitchen and the rooms above it, I told myself, as I climbed up the spiral staircase to the Muniment Room.

I thought of myself behind the thick walls on freezing winter nights, with the ruins all round me, in the moonlight. I have always wanted a little house built in the heart of wonderful ruins. At school it had been the corner of a Greek temple, where I grew plants and had a window in a wall contrived between the drums of two huge Doric columns.

I looked at the prints and the records in the Muniment Room, and thought of the pictures and the treasures of the house crackling in the flames.

Outside again, I looked at the outhouses, the laundry, the brewery, the stables and then, after gazing at some stairs which seemed to lead down to a cellar, I left the place with all its crusted history and started on my day's journey.

Being so stiff and sore, I decided to go no more than a few miles. I remembered my great-aunt and uncle and their daughter, who lived at Petersfield. I had not seen them since I was nine years old, when I and my mother had stayed with them for a week or two in the autumn. I remembered how I had tried to paint the coloured leaves and holly in the gardens, and how the daughter, Marjorie, had invited me to a fudge and toffee-making in her sitting-room one wet and misty afternoon. I remembered watching her pouring the thick condensed milk into the saucepan, and how I hoped that I wouldn't taste the tin when the fudge was made. Of course to me she was quite old, twenty-four or twenty-five. I did not like the way she did her hair in two buns over her ears.

I wondered, now, as I walked along, whether I should call on them and cadge a bed for the night. 'They won't know who I am until I've explained,' I thought. I wondered if I could brave it out, or whether it seemed too insolent. They were really such distant relations and my family had only kept in touch with them once a year, at Christmas.

I passed a lot of children playing in the road under the shade of a large-leafed tree. For some reason they struck me; it may have been the colour of their clothes under the heavy green shade. I thought of this moment in the cruel, romping, dirty children's lives. 'I've caught it in my mind for ever,' I thought. 'They'll all grow up and get diseased and die; but I shall remember them always like this.'

Just outside Petersfield I sat down in the long grass at the side of the road and eased the rucksack off my back. My bright blue shirt was stuck to my skin with sweat. I pulled it off and flapped it to and fro to fan my flesh and to dry it. I decided to look up my great-uncle's address in the telephone book, as I could not remember it. I went in search of a booth and soon found one, luckily. Next I found the address, and then asked a passer-by the way.

As I walked down the drive I felt horribly self-conscious and at a disadvantage. I could not imagine what my reception would be like; and yet I felt that it was cowardly not to make use of these convenient relations when I was so in need of somewhere for the night.

I found my uncle alone; my aunt and cousin had gone out to some sale-of-work in a friend's garden. I hurriedly and confusedly explained about myself and how I could not walk any farther that day.

He asked me about my father, who was his real nephew; then he said rather diffidently, as if he felt that, young as I was, yet even I might object to so outrageous a hint, 'Of course, there are buses.'

My face went red and I became very flustered and angry and more determined than ever to dig my toes in.

'I really am terribly tired,' I said. 'It would be marvellous if I could just stay here for the night and rest.'

'Of course, of course,' he said correctly, with no feeling at all.

Tea was brought in, on a large silver tray with kettle and tea caddy. I tried very hard to make out the crests winking on all the glistening pieces, for at home I had a book with two Bois crests in it and I wondered which one my uncle used, or whether he had something quite different – even of his own manufacture, I added maliciously, thinking of the hint about the buses.

I could not crane my neck and stare indefinitely at the silver, so I took a scone and started to talk as pleasantly as I could to my uncle. Presently my aunt and cousin came in, and my uncle said, rather repressively, 'Oh, this is Denton, who's on a walking tour and he's going to spend the night with us.'

My aunt gave me a sharp, quick look, then dowsed it. Her white hair and the blue velvet bow under the rim of her hat looked mild, but her face didn't.

'Oh, how nice,' she said, with no colouring in her words. I began to feel that they all thought my behaviour extraordinary.

'Oh, we saw you sitting in the grass at the side of the road,' my cousin said. 'I remember that blue shirt but I didn't know it was you of course.'

I was taken out on to the terrace to look at the magnificent view. The house was built on the ridge of a steep hill. The garden fell away in terraces.

Afterwards I looked into the drawing-room and remembered the ugly satin-wood cabinets filled with curiosities which I had loved as a child. I now thought them shoddy and dull – the Japanese ivories – horrible. The Persian helmet with its veil of chain-mail still hung above the staircase. I had believed my uncle before when he had told me that it was probably some Crusader's; now I felt that it, with many others, must have been manufactured specially to hang above the staircase in the houses of people like my uncle.

That night I went up to my room thankfully. I was sorry that I had come, yet glad that I should have a comfortable bed and that I should have to pay nothing for it. I tried to read but could not concentrate, so I turned out the light and fell asleep.

The first thing in the morning I began to worry about the tip to be left in my room. Was two shillings enough? I hoped very much that it was; it seemed far too much to me. But then I knew that I was a biased judge and that my sudden appearance must have been disconcerting.

We all sat in the dining-room talking quite pleasantly. They had evidently got over their surprise at my descent. They seemed to accept me as something rather odd but fairly inoffensive. At the end of the meal my Aunt Maggie made signs at my Uncle Percy to take me on to the terrace. It appeared that one of the maids had given notice and that my aunt and Marjorie were going to help the rest of the household by clearing the table.

'Can't I help?' I asked, grabbing up something and taking it to the service hatch.

'No, no,' my aunt said hurriedly, almost angrily. 'Go out with Percy on to the terrace, we can manage much better without you.'

I was amazed and rather hurt at not being allowed to make myself useful to them when I had made them useful to me.

Can she be so ridiculous as to be ashamed of clearing her own table before me? Or is it just her old-fashioned idea that males cannot do anything in the house and that it is wrong, almost indecent, for them to offer to help?

I went out with my uncle on to the terrace and we walked down into a sort of water garden with clipped yews and an old lead cistern. The trimness, the flagged walk and the leaded panes of the house were all very much the businessman's idea of home. It looked very prosperous and dull and soothing.

'We're trying to sell it,' my uncle said gloomily. 'Too big for just Maggie and me and Marjorie, now that the others have flown, but would you believe it, we can't get an offer that will anything like cover all the money we've spent on it. Why, the garden was a wilderness and look at it now!'

'That's always the way, isn't it?' I said as comfortably as possible.

'Other people only see the results, they don't know what's gone into it.'

We walked to the edge of the wood still exchanging platitudes; then I went back to my bedroom, left the two shillings rather reluctantly, and came down again to say good-bye.

They were all pleasant and distant and half-dead; so I made my escape and did not breathe again freely until I was in the road.

How stuffed and stuck in the mud people are! I thought. They ought to have enjoyed having me and told me to come again. I remembered that I should write a thank-you letter to my aunt, but because I did not know whether to spell Maggie with a 'y' or 'ie' I felt that I should probably never do it. And I never did.

That night I arrived in Winchester. I was tired but I had walked off some of my aching; I was beginning to feel broken in. This was to be my first night in a Youth Hostel. I followed the directions in my little booklet and found the front door to the City Mill down the narrow side street. Before finding the right turning I had looked from the stone balustraded bridge in the main street, and seen the old red-tiled mill crouching over the clear rushing water.

It seemed an exciting place to spend the night in. I knocked rather nervously on the door and was let in by a stocky young woman with very short hair.

'Nobody knocks here,' she said gaily and rather boisterously. 'I'm the warden,' she explained. 'I'll show you where everything is.'

I found myself liking her, although I doubted if she would altogether like me. She seemed to accept me as I was, with no more questions, which was reassuring.

'This is where you can cook,' she said, leading me into a low dark room, fitted up with many gas-rings round the wall.

'Or if you don't want to do your own meals, we'll make something for you,' she added.

'Oh, I've got some food already in my rucksack,' I said.

'Good, less trouble for us,' she answered. She took me up a ladder-staircase and when she had pulled the sacking curtain away at the top I found myself in a huge barn with windows on two sides and a large open fire-place. There were tables, chairs, some tattered books and maps on the walls.

'This is the Common Room. It separates the sheep from the goats,' she said archly. 'The sheep sleep up in that loft.' She pointed to one end of the room where another ladder-staircase led up to a dark, curtained region. 'And the goats sleep in the dormitory through here.' She led me across the room, into a bare windy shed where iron beds stood in rows.

'Underneath are the men's wonderful washing arrangements; come and see.' She took me down below the dormitory. The sound of the rushing water came up to meet us. 'Go in there,' she said, pointing to a door. 'I won't, because they've probably none of them got a stitch on.'

She chortled, and left me staring at the door. I opened it and saw a mass of pink bodies laughing and dancing about as they stood in the middle of the rushing water, holding on to a stout rope.

The river passed right through the building here, under two shallow arches. The room was simply a covered-in section of river, with two bricked and beaten-mud banks and a rope from wall to wall, on to which the bather-washers had to cling because of the swiftness of the current.

'Don't let go, lad,' someone yelled out ribaldly. 'You don't want to be washed out in front of the public bridge. There's always plenty of watchers leaning over to see what they can see.'

I laughed, and started to pull my clothes off hurriedly. The atmosphere was exciting and gay. I wanted to feel the clear white water tearing past me. The people washing and shaving in the enamel basins ranged along one wall seemed tame and rather sordid.

I jumped in and was almost knocked over by the current. I grabbed desperately at the rope, caught it, and then had time to feel the wonderful, clear, biting coldness of the water. Its mad racing gave it the tingle of soda-water.

'What did I tell you, lad,' the same person cried out to me again. 'You were nearly washed out in your birthday suit; then I suppose you'd have expected me or someone else to come and rescue you.'

I looked up at him and saw that he was a big red-skinned man with ginger hair. The clash in his colouring and the water pouring off his huge limbs made him look absurd and rather likeable. I smiled and laughed and danced about in the water, but never letting go of the rope for a moment. Under the arch I could just see the foot of the bridge, and when I put my face down to the surface of the water I could see the people and the traffic passing over it.

Someone else was talking to me now. I turned round and saw a young man almost bald, with very thick creamy skin, dark eyes and rather rabbit-like teeth.

'Terrific current,' he said, in what are known as cultured tones.

I agreed and said how much I enjoyed the water after my day's walk. He asked me how far I'd come, and seemed very eager to have someone to talk to.

When we had both got out and were drying our hair and bodies in one corner of the room I noticed that he stuttered rather badly.

When we were in the water the noise had been too much to notice anything more than the general shape of his words. I thought with rather a conventional pang of annoyance that I always attracted rather dreary oddities and not the interesting people that I wanted to know. Then I tried to stifle this unpleasant feeling and listened to him with more attention. He was asking me which way I meant to go on the next day. I said, towards Salisbury.

'Oh great, perhaps we could walk together,' he suggested. 'I'm going that way too.'

I knew that I would have to walk with him, but I felt doubtful and unhappy about it. Physically he was certainly repellent, and his eager, stuttering, cliché talk would become very tiring.

I smiled at him and said that that would be fine; then I left him and went to cook my evening meal on one of the gas-rings in the low kitchen.

Others were already there, running about with frying-pans and kettles in their hands. I got out the eggs and tomatoes I had bought. I dropped a large lump of butter into the saucepan and threw on two eggs and some peeled tomatoes; then I made cocoa with the rich milk I'd bought, and rushed my meal up to the common-room on a crazy tin tray.

I was delighted with my own cooking, as I always am. The deliciousness of the scrambled eggs and tomatoes, and afterwards the cocoa with biscuit and jam and a chocolate bar, made me utterly contented and happy. I began to read one of the tattered books, and felt that this Youth Hostel, at least, was a pleasant place.

After my meal, when the lights began to appear on the bridge across the stretch of river, I grew restless at being indoors and wanted to go to explore the town. The warden shouted after me as I went out of the front door, 'We lock up at ten, so don't be late, else you'll have to sleep in the ditch.'

I walked up the narrow lane to the main street and looked up and down. People were parading in couples and talking and laughing. I knew that the cathedral would be closed, so I walked by the banks of the Itchen until I came to an iron seat. I sat down and for some reason I began to think of red crayfish. I don't know why, perhaps I remembered that I had once been told that they were caught in rivers. A huge yellow moon began to rise and cast its oily wriggles of light on the water. It was a magic moment, with the lovers talking softly and laughing near me in the dark.

A man came up and sat down on the other end of the seat. He lit a cigarette and I saw that he had a silk scarf round his neck. 'Some night!' he said with emphasis, blowing out the smoke and stretching his legs forward, so that they were stiff.

He seemed bored and dissatisfied, and said, 'Purple passion!' when a particularly loud giggle and kiss were wafted to us. He seemed to be laughing at the lovers, yet I knew that he wished to be one himself. He told me that he was in the army and that he was home on leave. We walked on a little way forlornly. He said that he would show me a different way back to the City Mill. He led the way up a steep bank and gave me a hand as I slipped backwards over the crumbling earth. We pushed on through the bushes and I think we came out somewhere near the school. I seem to remember its grey walls shimmering under the moon, on the other side of the water.

He told me the way to the Mill and I said goodbye hurriedly, feeling that it must be getting late. I left him standing by the water, hunching his shoulders disconsolately and wondering what he should do for the rest of the evening.

I ran back through the streets and arrived at the Mill just before ten. A moment afterwards I heard it striking from some tower. People were already in bed in the dormitory. I unpacked my sheet sleeping-bag and put it between the hostel blankets. I had no pillow but that did not matter, I always slept with my head low.

Furtively I slipped off my shorts and jumped into bed in my shirt. When in bed I discovered that my neighbour was an American. He leaned across and affably asked me questions, about what I was studying, what my father did, where I was heading for.

He was interested when I said that my father was in China, and seemed to take it for granted that he was in the Diplomatic Service. I told him that my father was a director of rubber companies, and wondered if this would make him feel less interested, but it did not seem to. He told me of his impressions of England, of the awful socks and underclothes he'd had to buy, because there were no others. I found myself becoming a little ruffled and annoyed, and was careful to explain that although my mother was also an American from Boston, yet I did not find the English clothes so very much worse than the American – in many ways I thought them decidedly better. I underlined this rather snobbishly, I think, fixing my mind as I spoke on the difference between a pair of English trousers and a pair of American 'pants'.

Someone shouted exasperatedly to all the people who were still talking, 'Oh, do shut up.' And I suddenly remembered with a pang my own agony at school when I could not go to sleep because of the droning voices of the others. I would talk no more to my American companion, and fell asleep soon, lulled by the roaring of the water as it dashed between the arches underneath us.

I dropped my ivory comb on the concrete floor, in the morning, and broke one of its teeth which enraged me. But I dashed down again into the racing mill-stream and forgot it.

After breakfast the nearly-bald stutterer (whom I must call Williams as I have forgotten his real name; this might even be it – in any case it was a name of that type) came up to me smilingly and asked when I wanted to start. I suggested that we should first go to look at the cathedral, and we left the hostel together, telling the warden that we both hoped to come again to the City Mill.

I could not really enjoy the cathedral with Williams. I had seen it all before, but I decided that on my return journey I should come to it again, and this time alone.

We stared at Jane Austen's tomb and at Professor Tristram's reconstructed murals. We gazed at the black carved font and at the Norman arches, always so much more impressive to casual visitors.

Outside in the sunlight and warmth again, I felt more friendly to Williams. He was talking to me animatedly the whole time and I found for once that I had very little to do but listen.

We left the town behind us and started to go down a narrow lane, which we had looked up on our maps. It led at first between suburban houses, but soon ran over a wide wind-swept plain. The cloud-shadows raced across the grass and my companion started to tell me all about Eric Linklater's *Juan in America*. He almost became inarticulate when he described how the woman lion-tamer took Juan up in her mouth and held him over the banisters, about to drop him down the staircase well. I was amazed that he could tell me a story from a book at this length.

We passed a wonderful beech wood and a huge field of some green vegetables; then we came to a stone obelisk on a hill. I insisted on going up to read it and, of course, cannot remember now what it was all about. I feel it was a private monument to some old general, or was it perhaps to commemorate some disaster?

Williams now began to tell me of his family. He explained that his hair began to fall out the year before, when it was very hot and his grandmother was 'kicking the bucket' in the tiny London flat.

'The doctor says it's due to nervousness and because of the heat and the strain of having my grandmother like that in the next room,' he said.

Now it may have been stupid, but at that time I did not know what 'kicking the bucket' meant. I did not realize for some moments that she had been dying. I could not completely understand his story, and heard with disgust that he was ordered to cover his scalp with castor oil every day.

'Is it beginning to grow again?' I asked politely.

'Oh, yes; I hope soon to have a thick crop.'

I said nothing more, for I saw no sign of it. We were now passing a long range of gnarled sloe bushes. I imagined them later in the year, bearing their heavy load of dusty blue fruit.

We sat down to eat our lunch. My companion produced unappetizing food and ate it with no discrimination at all. One moment it was there and the next moment it was not there – that was all. He took all I offered him of my own and swallowed it in the same way.

So far we had walked entirely in the open country, following rutted lanes and narrow foot-paths; but after our meal we struck a road which led into a small village. A goose was walking in the road and the rattling bus, as it came along, ran over the goose and stopped with a jerk. I was sickened and turned away, but not before I had seen the goose subside and squat on the road, as if it were resting. It turned back its meek, long-suffering, stupid head in a way that seemed to express its acceptance of the incident as something quite in order.

I was horrified and said something to Williams. I heard a woman say, 'Oh, poor thing; they oughtn't to drive so fast in the village.' We walked on hurriedly, not looking at the mark on the road, as soon as someone had taken the goose away. It was still alive. Oh, how I wished they'd kill it!

Nether Wallop was the charming name of the village we were aiming for. A hostel was marked on one of the main roads which crossed the plain. Soon we were on the edge of the whistling telegraph-wire country. The hostel was a shack. One of those 'good-pull-in' places where lorrymen and drivers eat huge pasties. The sleeping quarters were in another hut, some distance from the other, and off the road. The woman who took us across to it smiled, and I thought what lovely teeth she had, until I realized they were all false. They gleamed and glistened in such pretty regular rows. She really was a charming woman, her small head, dark hair and concentrated, compact little body were full of so much animation. She seemed delighted to see us, laughed and joked, and asked us all sorts of questions.

The sleeping hut was wonderfully neat and clean with rows of low little beds with bright blankets. The flimsy beaver-board walls seemed to give me a sense of security; I suppose because they made me realize clearly what wind and weather were on the other side.

We left our rucksacks on our beds and went back with the woman to the other hut. A large young A.A. man had come in and was sitting rather impatiently at one of the tables. The woman immediately went to a corner, where there was an oil stove, and began to cook him three eggs and four rashers of bacon in a frying-pan. When she brought the cooked eggs and the sizzling bacon to him, still in the frying-pan, the A.A. man turned to me and, slapping his hands together dramatically, said, 'That's something like, isn't it! Give a man a meal like that when he's been on the road all day!' He cut a huge slice of bread and started to wolf the eggs and bacon silently.

I went up to the counter and bought a bar of chocolate. I slipped out, leaving Williams behind, and ate my chocolate in the fields, where I watched some children playing.

The night was noisy and troubled in the hut. The wind beat against the thin walls and made the windows squeak, and Williams snored slightly. But I felt happy and contented, although I lay awake. The next morning I contrived to lose Williams. I think I managed it by saying that I wanted to see Amesbury, which was not on the way to Salisbury. I left him outside the hut; we both smiled affably and said we hoped we'd meet later in the journey. I was in terror that he would suggest accompanying me to Amesbury, for I could not tell which book he would choose to describe in detail to me today.

I passed many army lorries on the road and Amesbury itself seemed full of khaki. I went into the abbey-church and sat staring for some time at the carving of a mitred head. The nose was broken and the whole thing seemed so full of ancientness and magic for me that I loved it. The dusty sunlight from a window bathed and played about it in heavy liquid spots; and a shining bluebottle teased and buzzed, settling now on the broken nose, now on the curls of the beard.

I sat there reading some of the history of the place which the vicar had so thoughtfully provided. I learnt about Gay and the Duchess of Queensberry. I thought of the apron which she would insist on wearing on all party occasions.

Leaving the church I went and stood on the bridge and looked towards the house where they'd lived. I could see very little; so after a few more moments of gazing I decided to set out for Salisbury.

The hostel there was again a mill, but the whole atmosphere was very different. It was at West Hownham just outside the city, in fields split up and divided by streams. I walked down a tarred path under willows, evidently a promenade for the city families and lovers. At one point one passed over a white bridge. Water-lily leaves covered the water under it, giving the impression that the buttercup richness of the fields had overflowed the banks. When I saw the medieval flint-work of the Priory Mill I felt delighted. The hard, glistening squares, so neatly put together and framed in stone, gave me pleasure. A painted sign hung out from the front of the building. I noticed that the sign had glass over it, which struck me as wrong and inappropriate.

At the door some smart waitresses met me. They still wore their stiff gauzy caps, but they were pulling them off as fast as they could and it was clear that they were going home for the night. They laughed and joked between themselves, but took no notice of me. At last, when they had all gone, a large lady in black came towards me. Her manner seemed harassed, but there were attempts at graciousness.

'Have you come to spend the night at the hostel?' she asked.

I said, 'Yes,' and she told me that it was in a building behind.

'But first let me show you my mill,' she said.

She took me into a long, pleasant tea-room and then upstairs, where the roof sloped and there was a large grand piano.

'Pachman's,' she said, waving her hands towards it carelessly. 'He's often played on it to me, so when he died I bought it.'

She went on to tell me how Augustus John and many other famous people came to her mill. She told me who had done the inn sign, but I have forgotten the name and it did not convey anything to me then. I realized now why it was glassed over, but I still thought it very dull.

The lady was now talking about the people who used the Youth Hostel.

'Such nice young people,' she said. 'Such a nice type, really quite educated sometimes.'

This compliment was more than I could swallow. I felt hot and insulted and longed to tell her a great many things about myself, which only very vulgar people find it possible to mention. I stood in frustrated silence, waiting to be shown the hostel quarters.

'You'll find everything you want inside that door,' said the lady, pointing to an adjoining early-Victorian house built out at the back of the mill. I saw her locking doors and collecting keys, and I suddenly realized that she was about to leave for the night. I would be entirely alone, unless some other walkers appeared.

'Oh, you don't live here then,' I said, liking her and wishing for her company more than I would have believed possible a moment ago.

'No,' she answered, placidly going about her business and not noticing my feeling.

'It's going to be rather gloomy here, all alone. I hope there are no ghosts of monks,' I said cheerfully.

'Oh, I expect you'll be all right,' she said. Then she was gone, clanking her keys as she walked away. I was left alone to enter the squalid-looking Victorian house. I looked into the first room, where there was nothing but a battered oil-stove. I remembered that the lady had told me that nothing was quite finished yet – it was only just begun. I climbed up the dry, worm-eaten steps and found myself in the chief bedroom. A sagging double-bed stood there, nothing else. There were bolsters and dark blankets on it, that appeared to me then unbelievably sinister.

I decided to explore no farther. I felt that the best thing to do was to get into bed and try to fall asleep before the light had entirely faded, and to pray that one slept all night. The thought of waking in that horrible room at dead of night was unnerving.

I wondered what had happened to Williams. I longed for him to appear, but knew that he never would.

Looking at the pale square of light from the window, as I lay wrapped in the blankets on that grim bed, I told myself stories, threw my mind back to pleasant things until at last I did fall asleep.

I woke up once not knowing exactly where I was. When I remembered, it was worse than not knowing. I thought of the worm-eaten stairs and the passage outside the door; then I tried desperately to burrow down into sleep again.

I did not wait for the lady of the house in the morning. I paid my shilling to one of the waitresses and disappeared as soon as possible.

I reached Shaftesbury early that afternoon. I saw its name Shaston written on several old milestones, which we shall now never see again. Climbing up to the old town I had the feeling that it was built on ramparts and terraces. I thought of Lord Shaftesbury and charity and, when I reached the top, I stood by some iron railings and wooden posts and gazed at the view for a long time. There was an attractive little house nearby, to let, and I wished that I could take it and furnish it and live there.

Afterwards I went to look at some ecclesiastical ruins but, from what I can remember, I could see very little.

I had my late lunch and then set out again, determined to reach Templecombe that evening.

The hostel there was housed in the outbuildings of an hotel. The sun was setting as I reached the converted country house. With its lights sparkling across the fields it looked grand and dignified and inviting. I went into the stable yard, feeling happy and satisfied, wanting my evening meal and bed. I saw the hostel notice and climbed up above the stable to a long bare dormitory. The floor was dirty, and dusty with chaff. Others were sitting on the beds or unpacking their rucksacks. They hailed me good-naturedly and I felt a glow of pleasure that I was not going to be alone as I was the night before.

I chose a bed and for some reason, which I cannot now remember, decided that I must have sheets. The reason may have been that my own sleeping-bag had become wet through being packed too close to my washing things (I had no sponge bag).

One of the others suggested that I should go and ask the manager of the hostel for them, saying that I would pay for them. I went to do this, humming happily as I crossed the stable-yard. Someone went to fetch the manager and I waited in a passage way.

He arrived – a plump little man with metal-rimmed glasses. Gradually he worked himself up into a fury over my request. His short arms swung out jerkily and his lower lip glistened with saliva.

'Sheets, sheets, what do you mean by asking for sheets!' he shrieked in his horrible voice.

I was amazed and also rather alarmed, for he seemed likely at any moment to strike me. I was as rude and insolent and arrogant as possible in return. I tried to say the things that would aggravate his sense of inferiority still further; but I will tell you now that I was frightened in spite of my rage. He seemed to me a mad demon of that most loathsome, petty tyrant sort. I pitied the poor servants who worked under him. I thought of the hell this type of reptile created around him.

'Of course I can't stay here another minute,' I said, as he screamed at me to get out. I turned my back on him abruptly, saying that I would write to the Secretary of the Youth Hostel Association about him; which was a stupid threat, as I knew that I would be too lazy ever to do so.

I told the others about the repulsive little man and slung my rucksack on my back again.

'Where are you going?' someone asked. 'It's getting late.'

'Oh, I'll walk on until I find a town or village,' I said carelessly. The rage had given me new energy, although the moment before I'd felt extremely tired.

I said good-bye and walked back on to the road again. It was almost dark now. I sang to myself and kept time with my feet, wanting to obliterate the horrible scene of meaningless spite and hate. It is only some time after such happenings that they begin to bite into one's consciousness and spoil one's peace. I was jarred and jolted by the unexpectedness of this onslaught.

Slowly a feeling of gaiety and adventure displaced the other. I was all alone, and it was night, and I had nowhere to sleep. It was a joke. I sang louder and louder, clapping my shoes on the road to make them *ring*. Seeing a warm light in a cottage window, and still being in this irresponsible mood, I went to the back door and knocked.

'Excuse me, but can you tell me of anywhere near here where I can spend the night?' I asked the woman, who held a candle up to me as I spoke. As at Wiston, I was willing her to say that I might sleep there; but again there was no result. She just looked at me doubtfully and shook her head, murmuring something about Wincanton.

I turned away angrily, saying to myself that English people were the most inhospitable and boorish on the face of the earth.

It must have been very late at night when I reached a sloping stone wall and started to climb the gradual hill up to Wincanton. Dark trees overhung the road, and everything that I could at all distinguish seemed made of stone. At the top of the hill, on the left side of the road, I saw a light in the window of a small pub. I went in, steeling myself for the refusal which seemed likely. A woman was mopping up the bar and emptying ash-trays. She looked at me suspiciously and asked several rather impertinent questions – where I had come from, and why I was so late. Not wanting to offend her I answered as pleasantly as possible. After what seemed like some time she took me rather sulkily up the stairs and showed me into a high, wide room with several white counterpaned beds in it. Then she left me, saying something about breakfast in the morning. I began to undress, hoping that I was going to have the room to myself; but just as I climbed into bed, the door opened and a fleshy early-middle-aged man burst into the room. Almost immediately he tore off his collar and tie. From his flushed face and heavy breathing I took it that he had been drinking. He flung off his clothes and got into bed naked. He did not seem even to have noticed me, and I lay very flat and still in my bed until I heard him snoring.

The suspicious woman gave me a well-cooked breakfast in the morning of fried eggs and coffee. I was surprised at the coffee, having expected black Indian tea. I paid her four shillings and thought that her inn was quite good in spite of her manner. I could not see the man of the night before anywhere; he must have gone out to his work early.

I went out to look at the yellow stone town of Wincanton, then walked on to Castle Cary, I think because I liked the name. From here my journey is lost; I can remember nothing until I emerged in the market place at Dunster. I do not understand this blank, but as I look at the map no name strikes any chord at all.

At Dunster I stared at that quaint columned market-cross, or whatever it is, and then pressed on to Minehead. The hostel was on a hill just behind the town. After I had found it and left my rucksack, I went down into the town to see the sights. The town seemed tawdry with white balconies, and pieces of paper floating in the air. The streets seemed littered with coloured paper from oranges, or the rind itself. I walked down the wide street to the sea, feeling dismal and gloomy. The sight of so many half-naked ugly people sitting in stolid rows on the beach did nothing to lighten my gloom. There seemed no joy anywhere.

I walked back into the town and who should I see suddenly but Miss Forman, who had taught me music at Repton. She was walking across the road. She stopped, recognized me and came up to speak. I was delighted; the dreary town, and being so much alone on my tramps, made the pleasure of seeing a friend intense.

'Hullo, what are you doing here?' she asked. She too seemed pleased to see me.

'I'm on a walking tour,' I said. We walked along together and I learnt that she was staying with her brother-in-law, who had been my headmaster but was now the Bishop of Chester.

'You must come back and have tea with us; he'd very much like to see you again,' she said decisively.

I trembled inwardly. I liked the headmaster, I even admired him; but I had run away from Repton and been sent back, and altogether had made a certain amount of trouble, and the remembrance of this made me self-conscious. My clothes too began to worry me; shorts and electric-blue shirt were not correct for tea with a bishop. I also felt rather dirty.

'Oh, thank you so much, but do you think he'd really like to see me?' I asked doubtfully.

'Of course, and my sister too.'

'Well, then, I'll just rush back to the hostel and wash and make myself a little more presentable before I appear. What is the address, so that I can find the house?'

I was given a little slip of paper and full directions; then I left her and ran all the way back to the hostel.

I found new arrivals sitting on their beds, when I entered the dormitory.

They don't know that I'm going to tea with a bishop, I said to myself. It seemed so rococo, and rather like the line of a rude limerick – going to tea with a bishop – except that it would be very difficult to rhyme it with anything.

I took out my other blue shirt, which was cleaner. I could have wished it to be sober white. I suddenly hated the bright, unrelieved, eye-confusing colour. I ran about in nothing but my shorts, washing my face and hands and legs, and trying to find a better pair of socks. I begged some shoe polish from one of the others, and at last set out with my hair as brushed and combed as possible.

I walked slowly, trying not to get hot and sweaty before I arrived. I really felt very nervous, and it showed itself in my exaggerated worrying about my appearance.

I found the house quite easily; it was on a hill dotted with other houses of the same type. They faced in various directions and were set in heavy clumps of trees and bushes. The effect was a crowded seclusion, if that can be imagined.

The front door was wide open. Miss Forman had seen me approaching, so she was there to meet me. I was taken into a long narrow room with windows looking down the hill. There was very little furniture about and the rugs on the floor were rucked up and at rather crazy angles, as if someone had been skidding and falling about.

The Bishop came in and welcomed me breezily. I noticed his huge episcopal ring; it fascinated me. I tried to see what was engraved on it. It looked like a mitre. The ring was of the shape called, I think, 'marquise', that is, two gothic arches joined together at their bases – a very lovely, graceful shape. The colour of the stone was deep purple – an amethyst, I suppose. He wore it on his index finger which seemed to make it all the more anachronistic and significant. I could not help smiling to myself at the difference between this ring and the rest of his appearance, so matter-of-fact and down-to-earth.

He began to ask me questions about my visit to China when I had left Repton, what I was doing now, and where my brothers were.

All the time we were talking two small nephews, who were staying in the house, ran about and slid on the floor, which explained the state of the rugs.

Someone rang the gong for tea and we went into the dining-room. I was surprised to see the enormous table and the number of chairs round it. I knew the Bishop had several sons but this would not explain so many seats. I was soon to be introduced to more nephews and some other older relations. Mrs Fisher was pouring out from a large teapot at the far end of the table, and the cups were being carried round by the two young nephews. Just as my cup had arrived at my place, I got up to be introduced to yet another person who had entered the room. The boy was holding the cup out from behind me and as I rose, not knowing that it was there, I caught it on my shoulder and sent the steaming water in a jet, the whole length of the long table. I was too horrified and confused to say anything; the cup was not broken, but there was the long brown stain, steaming on the table-cloth. The boy laughed and Dr Fisher, seizing a piece of bread, threw it down the table to his wife. She caught it deftly, still pouring out with the other hand.

Now the whole table was laughing and gay and boisterous; my awful accident had been merged and incorporated into the Bishop's wild bread-throwing. It really was the most charming and brilliant thing to do.

I was given another cup of tea and slowly began to recover some self-possession. I ate the bread and butter and jam and cakes, and thought how nice it must sometimes be to live in large families with all the noise and mess and pleasant human feeling. I had scarcely ever had it in my life. After tea the Bishop took me walking on the moor above the house. He talked about the Roman Catholics, and I listened interestedly. There was a story which I cannot properly remember about a priest who managed to buy a piece of land for a church, from a woman who had no intention of selling. It was all done very skilfully. I talked about the cathedrals which sprung up so close to Church of England ones. I asked if there were any particular method in this, and if so whether it helped the Roman Catholic cause much. I pointed out that very few people who were not Roman Catholics ever went down the side streets to Westminster Cathedral, although they could see its tower from miles away.

We parted, after he had invited me to travel over Exmoor in their car on the next day, as they were making a journey in that direction and it would help me on my way.

The next morning I was at the house punctually. There was a certain amount of bustling before we finally settled into the old car. Mrs Fisher drove and the Bishop and I sat behind. I think Miss Forman must have been in front with her sister, but I cannot remember any of the sons or nephews coming with us.

We were soon driving over the bare, dull moor with its carpet of lightly knitted little blueberry bushes. We passed some walkers, and the Bishop poked me and said, 'There is someone in a blue shirt, just like yours.' I was horrified to have attention drawn to my blue shirt. My hatred of it had grown even stronger, and I was determined that I would dye it on the first possible occasion.

Mrs Fisher was talking to her husband over her shoulder. There was some argument or joke about his old school, Marlborough. I suddenly imagined him in one of those old groups of football players, photographed in such stout and manly attitudes with tassels on their caps. I thought of what a lot he'd managed to achieve in his life and how nice it must be to be successful. He still seemed young and boisterous too, which made one feel that he had the best of everything.

I left them sorrowfully, when they branched off to go to their friend's house. I had so enjoyed being with people who knew me and accepted me without any questions. I think one only gets this feeling after many days with strangers.

The moor spread out on all sides of me. I looked at my map to see exactly where I was. The next hostel was somewhere near South Molton; I set out down the road which seemed to run in that direction.

After walking for an hour or so I left the road and dropped down to a little stream. Its rusty colour, when I reached it, surprised me. I took off my shoes and bathed my feet and paddled; the rings of cold water round my ankles refreshed me. I stooped down, cupped my hands and scooped up some of the water to drink. I wondered if the rusty brown would make it taste of iron, but I could tell no difference to ordinary water when I swallowed it.

Leaving the stream, I made my way back to the road, striking a different section of it; here, there were fields on the other side, and a

stag hunt was in progress, for I was just in time to see a knot of horse-
men and women, before they disappeared down the rough lane.

I walked on, wondering if I should see any more of the hunt. The
sound of horses' hooves made me turn round to find, just behind
me, a person who looked like a young farmer, on a huge horse. He
wore a cap, and a handkerchief round his thick neck. His face was
broad and red and pleasantly coarse, and his clothes were dirty and
worn very jauntily.

'Can you tell me which way they've gone?' he asked in his soft,
sing-song voice.

I pointed down the road, but he seemed in no hurry. He asked
me where I was heading for, and seemed generally curious about me.

Suddenly he slapped his horse and said, 'Wouldn't you like to
jump up and have a ride on her? Aren't you tired, walking?'

'Do you mean, ride pillion behind you?' I asked, very taken aback,
but rather pleased at the idea.

'That's right,' he said. 'You jump up.'

I approached the horse, slung my rucksack up to him, and was
about to try to struggle up behind, when he changed his mind and
told me to get up in front. He took his feet out of the stirrup, and
pulled me up with his hands. I now sat before him like a small child;
he was so large that he made me feel like that. I could smell his
clothes – the mingled tobacco, beer, horse and sweat that clung to
them; and I could tell how hot he was, for I was pressed hard against
him as he reached round me for the reins. I could even feel his heart
beating into my back.

'Is that all right?' he asked, straddling his legs a little farther apart,
so that I could sit more in the saddle. The leather creaked; I felt the
hard press of his thighs and legs along my own.

'Now, shall we go hunting?' he suggested.

'Could we, like this?' I asked, half pleased, half fearful. It seemed
an amazing adventure to me. I wondered if I'd be able to keep my
seat when we really started moving. The thought of jumping
hedges or walls thrilled me with horror, yet I hoped he might
attempt it.

We were still ambling down the rough road; just as I thought we
were about to turn into a field, to catch up the hunt, the young
farmer bent over me and said cajolingly but with a certain menace,

'What are you going to give me for the ride, it's worth something to you, the ride, isn't it?'

This was so new and so unpleasant a turn of events that I could only answer aggrievedly, 'Oh, I didn't know you wanted money.' I was very hurt, since I thought that he had picked me up entirely for fun and amusement; I was also rather alarmed, for I now seemed to be in his power. I could not see myself escaping from between these two huge arms or throwing myself off that horse with any success. I decided to take up as light and indifferent an attitude as possible.

'What do you want?' I said coldly. 'I've got very little money, so perhaps I'd better get off at once.'

'No, don't do that,' he said, holding me on firmly. 'You give me something,' he wheedled. 'It's worth it to you, isn't it?' The wheedling from the strong lusty man enraged me; everything had been spoilt by his trying to extract money, and I had been enjoying myself so much.

'Put me down now and I'll give you sixpence; I want to go on walking.'

'Sixpence, what's sixpence!' he exclaimed.

'We've only gone a few yards, and I'm not going any farther, since you want to be paid. I can't *pay*,' I said, stressing the word.

'Oh, come on, give me a bit more than that and I'll take you a long way.'

I did not answer, but held the sixpence over my shoulder, hardly expecting him to take it. When I felt his hand on mine, grasping the sixpence, I decided to jump down; avarice that would accept six-pence was too disgusting.

I got my feet both to one side, and then jumped. The horse was still moving, but very slowly. I landed on my feet and then fell back-wards over a little bush, which annoyed me. As I picked myself up, I held my hands out for my rucksack; he pretended not to notice, and I thought for one moment that he was going to gallop away with it. Filled with horror (for it contained everything I needed for my journey) I ran after the horse and said, 'Chuck me my rucksack please.' My voice sounded very firm and severe and artificial.

At last he turned round; he was smiling. 'Catch!' he said as he swung it out to me. I caught it by the straps. When I looked up again, I was just in time to see him hit his horse, making it break into a fast trot. 'Good-bye,' he shouted jovially, as he disappeared across the fields. I did not answer; I was trying to understand the whole episode.

That night I slept in a loft with two other youths. It was clean and whitewashed, with straw mattresses on the floor. We lay on the creaking canvas and talked far into the night.

I made my way from Exmoor to the edge of Dartmoor. I had yet another great-aunt in view to provide my next night's bed. She was the sister-in-law of the uncle I had stayed with at Petersfield, and she had a house not very far from Okehampton. She had spent a few days at my grandfather's house and had told me then to be sure to visit her if ever I were in Devonshire. She wrote her address on a piece of paper and gave it to me.

I had it with me now. The name of the house was something unpronounceable and Chinese, for my aunt had spent her early life in that country. I remembered her telling me that she and her daughter had designed the house between them; I wondered what it would be like.

It was not easy to find, for it was in no village or town. When at last I discovered it, quite late in the evening, I saw that it lay on the very edge of the moor. The setting was truly lovely – on three sides wild, rolling ground, tightly wigged with heather, a stone wall climbing up a hill and ending in a tumbledown shed which might have been a shrine – but the house was as hideous as white paint and turrets could make it. At each corner was a turret with an iron cross or weathervane on top. Windows all round showed heavy lace and draperies within. The Chinese name on the gate seemed to suit. The whole thing was such a woolly mixture and degradation of ideas that a name in quite unknown language seemed the most appropriate.

I walked up through the shrubs. All the things with various coloured leaves I did not like seemed to be growing there.

I rang the bell and waited. A rather harassed maid came to the door and I explained who I was, asking if my aunt were at home. The maid bustled away to fetch her and I was left to gaze at the hall. It was furnished with those tables that have little Chinese men in ivory inlaid into the tawny wood. On the tables stood aggressive, thrusting ferns with frilly leaves. They grew from brass vessels which are used as chamber-pots in India. I wondered if my aunt knew this.

I put the thought away when I saw her coming towards me. She looked just the same, with winking glasses held in her hand and far too many things pinned to her shapeless black dress. There were watches, brooches, pieces of lace and ribbon; yet the whole effect was gloomy, and dowdy in the extreme.

She greeted me in rather a dazed way, saying, 'Of course we must find a bed for you, only we're full up here. I must ask my daughter Kathleen.'

She took me into the drawing-room where her other guests were sitting with her daughter. They all gaped politely, but seemed to give me very little attention. The daughter said that I could have a room at her house, although she was not living there herself.

When I had time to look about me, the ugliness of the room almost numbed me. It was hardly possible to believe that it had been concocted by sane people. Nothing seemed to have any significance at all. The tinted photograph in the silver frame seemed just as useful or useless as the horrible tortured fire-irons. Nothing had a place, and so nothing could be in its place. The tide of photographs and hideous Worcester vases might have swept off the tables and swamped the floor without giving one a more uncomfortable feeling than they did already. The liver-coloured curtains and white net might have festooned themselves all over the ceiling and the lamp-bracket without causing a more inconsequent effect. It was a mad-house scene.

Looking down at the flaming, rude shapes on the bile-green carpet I listened to what the male guest was saying. It appeared that he and his sister were connections of my aunt's family, but I had never heard of them. The man looked in the early thirties. He had a flat pale face, fair hair, and wore glasses. I thought that I might like him, when he stopped telling donnish stories to amuse my aunt. She, meanwhile, was being made quite kittenish by the stupid jokes. Her daughter, watching for a pause in the conversation, inserted her anecdote about the farm labourer at the political meeting.

'I'd been talking for some time,' she began, 'and in the course of my speech I used the phrase "I'm only a plain woman", as one might on such an occasion.' Here she shrugged her shoulders a little too

modestly. 'As soon as I'd said the phrase, up jumped a big fellow in
the back of the room and shouted out, "That's a lie – you're not a
plain woman, you're a lovely lady."' She smiled with satisfaction at
the end of her story. I looked at her, wondering if she'd ever been
beautiful (she must have been nearly fifty at this time). But even if
she had been beautiful, which seemed extremely doubtful, I still
wondered how she dared tell such a story. It seemed asking for
trouble.

Suddenly my great-aunt, who must have heard this story many
times before, broke through the laughter with some high-pitched
remark of her own. She seemed very excited and her eyes were glistening with water. I did not hear the remark, but the other man did,
and it seemed to shock him. The smile left his face and a disdainful
and repressive look took its place.

'Don't be lewd, Auntie,' he said coldly, 'there's no cause for lewd-
ness.' He pronounced the 'u' sound very thinly, making the word
into something most unpleasant.

It was my turn to be shocked; I had been wondering for some time
whether my aunt were not a little senile (chiefly because of the
hideousness of her rooms); now I felt certain of it. I wondered what
dreadful words she had uttered. Coming from an old lady, dressed all
in black, a rude word or phrase would have far more significance and
power to disconcert than from any other type of person. I was glad I
had not heard, for even as it was my cheeks were scarlet and sweating.

My aunt, still crying with laughter and heaving like a not quite
extinct volcano, turned to her nephew and said, 'Don't be strict, like
a governess.' She dried her eyes and looked all round, babyishly, for
approval.

Her daughter rose to her feet, evidently thinking that it was time
for me to go to bed. 'Calm yourself, Mother,' she said firmly, then,
turning to me, 'Come along: I'll lead you up to the house and see
that you have everything you need.'

I said good-night to my aunt, and the other two followed us out
of the room. In the hall we collected an iron lantern with an electric
bulb in it, and started to walk on the edge of the moor, close to a
stone wall. We followed the tracks of sheep through the dwarfed,
wind-shaped bushes. Little piles of black droppings were everywhere,
shining like Pontefract cakes in the light of the lantern. The other

three began to talk quite animatedly. I liked them better, out in the open, away from that disgusting house.

Kathleen took me up through the dark house to a room on the top floor, overlooking the moor. The bed was already made, so all she had to do was to fetch me a towel. She told me that the caretaker slept down below, so that I would not be entirely alone. She said good-night and left me without telling me where the lavatory or bathroom were. I saw that there was a hand-basin in my room, but still, that would not fulfil every need, unless one became very uncivilized. I went to the window wondering if perhaps that might be more suitable for my purpose. The others saw me standing there, and called up softly, 'Good-night, sleep well.' I saw the lantern rocking gently until it disappeared round the bend of the wall.

In the morning I walked back to my aunt's house for breakfast. The moor now looked so enticing that I longed to be off, across it, leaving all houses behind. The air was softer, warmer, more milky than ever, and all the blended, tweed colours of the hills seemed to be floating on this haze.

I entered the fantastic hall and the maid took me to the dining-room. I was early, no one else was yet down. I looked with amazement at all the food on the sideboard. When the maid left me, I lifted the electroplate lids one by one: sausages, mushrooms, eggs, bacon, tomatoes, kippers. I thought of the poor cook, and felt that the list was almost disgusting; but this did not prevent me from digging into the tomatoes, eggs, and mushrooms, until had a greedy pile on my plate. As I ate hungrily, I thought it very pretentious of my aunt to keep up Edwardian breakfast practices. I hoped that she only did it when she had guests; I could not bear to think of her all alone with so many dishes of food in front of her, though I realized that the mental picture fitted perfectly the mad-house profusion of everything else in the terrible rooms.

The man and his sister came in, and then Kathleen, smoothing her grey dress and bringing with her an air of bustling and management.

'Have you got all you want?' she asked us all, rather reminding me of a colonel or a matron, making an inspection. My aunt followed her closely.

'Come on, Mother,' she said brightly. 'We've all begun.'

My aunt sat down and started to eat an egg.

'Did I ever tell you about the curate who came to stay with us when we were girls?' she asked, turning specially to me. The others evidently had heard the story before; they went on talking.

'Well, the vicar had asked my mother to put this curate up for a night or two – there was to be some conference or something. We all wondered what he'd be like for several days before he arrived. I'd privately decided that he'd be very high-church and very good-looking. You can judge how disappointed I was when I saw him; his ears stuck out, he wore steel-rimmed glasses, and to cap all, he was extremely low-church.

'Next morning at breakfast I could hardly bring myself to talk to him. I noticed that my mother was making signs at me but at first decided to ignore them; then I looked down and saw that a big black fly was sitting in the very middle of the curate's fried egg. He started on the very edge of the white and was gradually working in to the yolk.

'In spite of my mother's signs, which were becoming almost frantic by now, I decided to do nothing. I just watched as that curate worked nearer and nearer to that black fly. He was far too short-sighted to notice it, and with the last mouthful he put it in his mouth and swallowed it. I wasn't going to warn such a creature, who had disappointed me so.'

My aunt ended on a note of girlish triumph painful to hear. The story was so very unpleasant and so very improbable that I did not know quite what to say. My one idea now was to escape.

'You'll need something to take with you, won't you?' asked Kathleen from her place. I thanked her and she got up and went to the sideboard; there, she cut large pieces of bread, and said, 'What would you like to put between them?' But without waiting for an answer she started to heap sausage, egg, tomato on to a slice of bread, squashing another piece on it. She made several of these huge sand-wiches, then told the maid to find her some grease-proof paper, and handed me the parcel with a sweet smile. 'That ought to keep you going,' she said heartily.

I thanked her, I thanked my aunt; I almost thanked the man and his sister in my eagerness to get away. They waved good-bye to me at the front door as I made straight across the moor. 'Don't get bogged,' was Kathleen's last cheerful warning.

To get away and to rid myself of the flavour of the house was my one idea. I walked up the hill where the stone wall led to the ruined shed. Sheep were everywhere, bleating and chewing degradedly. They made a dirty place of the charming hill, but their bells tinkled prettily and there was something patriarchal about their faces.

I sat in the ruined shed and gazed across the moor for some time. There seemed to be a curious shaped rock, crowning one of the hills in the distance. I decided to walk straight across the moor to it and eat my lunch in its shadow. Running down the hill, I found a sheep path and began to follow it in the direction of the hill; but it soon lost itself and I was left to pick my way as best I could.

After some time I struck a patch of quaking, bubbling ground; as I stood on a tussock, the brown bubbles burst round my feet. I became alarmed, remembering all the stories I had ever heard of men being sucked down by bogs. I walked round the edge of the treacherous piece, hoping to be able to skirt it. At one point I had to jump from tussock to tussock; they swayed a little from side to side as I landed, but otherwise were solid enough.

I left the bog behind me, gladly enough, and turned my face towards the rock again. If I found no more bogs in my way, I would soon be there.

At last I climbed up and leant my back against the flat slab. The wind was blowing but it was hot; I seemed the only person on the whole face of the moor. Taking out Kathleen's parcel, I unfolded the grease-proof paper and looked at the sandwiches. They had not travelled very well; the egg and the tomato had bulged out and burst through the bread in places. I took a large bite and, at the first taste, saw the breakfast table very clearly with my aunt telling her stupid story. I tried to follow my journey across the moor from the ruined shed. I thought I saw it shimmering in the distance, but as I looked I saw something else as well. A band of people seemed to be approaching; I could see a bobbing white shirt and something red.

As I munched my food I watched the group until I could make out four figures. They seemed to be coming straight towards me. I thought of them as two girls and two men, until I was finally able to see that they were all women. Two of them wore shorts and two tweed skirts.

They climbed up to me, laughing and talking noisily.

'Now we know,' the largest and boldest said.

'Know what?' I asked politely.

'Which you are. All the way across the moor we've been laying bets; man, woman, man. It's really been quite exhausting. We haven't been able to tell until this last minute.' I felt rather embarrassed.

'How queer,' I said, 'because I've been wondering about you too, as I watched you. I'd paired you off as two men and two girls.'

They all laughed, as if this were an uproarious joke; and I did notice then that one of the girls, at least, looked masculine. She was the one who had spoken first; her hair was short and she had a full face with heavy eyelids. She was not one of the ones wearing shorts, but her tweed skirt had something very workmanlike about it. She swaggered too; one could tell that she was the leader of the party.

We all sat down together to eat our lunch. I offered the remains of my sandwiches rather tentatively, but they all said that they had more than enough of their own. I learnt that they were staying nearby and went walking every day. I found myself wondering if they really were lesbians. The bold one seemed to treat me as a joke. She was quite good-natured, but I was obviously not to be taken seriously in her eyes.

I left them there, still eating. They all called out and waved to me as I walked away. I wondered what all the laughter was about and decided that it was about me.

Almost as soon as I was on the other side of the hill I found myself on the edge of another bog. That there should be a bog on the side of a hill amazed me. I could not understand why the water did not drain away. Again I jumped nervously from clump to clump of coarse grass. At one point I thought I was quite surrounded. I thought of calling out to the four girls, but decided that they would laugh even louder if they discovered me in difficulties. I jumped and sank in over my ankles. Jerking my feet out and almost leaving my shoes behind, I floundered on till I reached a firm part.

How I hated the bog! It had not swallowed me whole, but the very thought of it was horrible. My wet feet squelched in my shoes. Gradually the black mud dried into a hard case round my ankles.

I had come to the edge of the moor again, where there were stone walls and green fields. Before nightfall I must find the hostel, somewhere near Gidleigh.

When I did arrive, I found the wooden hut at the back of the farm-house full of small boys. A young master was in charge of them. He came up to speak to me at once, telling me that they had come from a school in the north and that they always went for a jaunt in the summer.

The boys were rushing around, shouting and making such a noise with their feet in the flimsy shed that I could hardly hear what he said.

'We've got to have supper now,' he yelled; and he went off cheerfully to marshal his boys.

He seemed very strict and full of orders, I thought. The boys were not particularly obedient, and I heard him shout exasperatedly, 'That's not playing the game – do it properly – don't play the goat,' many times.

The boys were perfectly sure that he would not get too angry. They banged about with enamel plates and mugs; a group of them hung round him continually, waiting for orders, but doing nothing.

At last he had them all sitting at the trestle table with their bread and butter and cocoa before them. He appealed to their better natures, telling them not to be greedy or to eat nastily. All the time he was working very hard; his dark hair began to hang down limply over his white, damp forehead, and his mouth was continually open.

The boys shouted all their jokes to him, asked him absurd questions, hung on his arms, and passed him food.

After the meal, when they had banged and rattled all the mugs and plates into the sink and wiped them on their dirty towels, they grouped round him in a spreading mass; the whole floor seemed to be covered with boys. An amazing silence reigned. What was going to happen? Were they going to pray?

The young master sat above them on the trestle table, swinging his feet. Several boys climbed up from the floor and clung around him. He shook them off half-heartedly, then decided to take their arms in his and hold them in subdued positions in this way.

'What's it going to be?' he asked all the boys with verve.

They shouted different names; the master decided on the most popular and called out:

'Very well, we'll have "Chestnut Tree".'

A roar of delight went up followed by as sudden a silence; then the singing and miming began.

The master led with athletic energy. He beat his chest, tapped his head, held out his hands, till the sweat grew in diamonds on his face. The chorus of piping shrill voices affected me curiously. It was such a green, unfeeling, assured sound. It was like listening to a roomful of green parrots who knew that they were saying their pieces properly. It was a charming sound, but also very indifferent and cold.

Towards the end of the song I noticed the farmer and his wife creeping into the room. They sat down quietly by the window and listened.

The boys had to rest for a moment after the 'Chestnut Tree'. Some sprawled full-length on the floor and kicked their legs in the air. Others started wrestling, rolling over and over till they were covered with dust. The more facetious trod on their neighbours and then offered elaborate apologies in what were supposed to be 'Oxford' accents.

The master looked at his watch, then called them to order. They all sat up straight and put on serious faces, for now it was to be the 'Londonderry Air'.

The master conducted gently and absently with one hand. As he waved it to and fro, and with his abstracted gaze, he looked as if he were trying to weave some spell. His rather prominent dark eyes were turned upwards and his whole head was thrown back a little, so that one saw the Adam's apple moving in his throat. With his free hand he clutched one or two of the boys to him, until they wriggled with pleasure at being trapped so tightly to his side. The dark eyes were glistening now and the black curly hair quivered on his damp forehead. The whole scene seemed one of most extraordinary fervour to me.

I saw the farmer's wife gazing far into the distance; her mouth was set and her plump, rather mottled cheeks held firm. She wore the tragic look of someone who is enjoying an unhappy feeling. Her eyes began to brim and sparkle, then I saw the tears running down her face. She took no notice, but left them there, glistening like shiny snail tracks. Her husband sat stolidly at her side, not looking at her, and the boys were too busy singing. I think I was the only one who saw.

I got up to go out, feeling angry at the sight of her tears. Crossing the yard, I walked into the front garden where coarse ferns grew between grey rocks. Up above me, on a hillock, a ruined wall and an archway showed above the tops of trees. I tried to reach the ruin, but tangled undergrowth and fencing barred the way wherever I tried to enter.

Another man, just arrived, joined me. We both stood looking at the forbidden hillock, wondering what its history was.

There was so much pandemonium in the morning that I decided to leave without making any breakfast. I said good-bye to the master as he tore by me with a frying-pan in his hand.

'Good-bye,' he said, squeezing my hand very hard, pressing the bones brutally together. 'They're good lads, aren't they?' he added anxiously, afraid, it seemed, that I was about to make some criticism. I agreed, and left him mobbed and besieged by the hungry boys.

I walked towards Chagford, hoping to have my breakfast there. The morning promised a wonderful day; heat-mist hovered over the moor and made the white houses in the little town shimmer. I looked at rather a large hotel and, after a little deliberation, decided to go in. The bright housekeeper met me in the hall.

'Yes, sir,' she said with a pleasant smile, 'breakfast will soon be ready. Would you care to wait in here?' She opened the door of a little room with magazines on the table. I sank down in the brown velour armchair and picked up one of those red and blue papers, perhaps the *Illustrated London News* or the *Tatler*.

She had not worried about the caked mud on my shoes and socks or my general ragamuffin air. How nice it was not to be stared at by insolent servants!

The gong boomed. I went quickly into the dining-room and sat down in the window. Hotel rolls and coffee delighted me after so many meals made by myself. I listened to the conversation of other breakfasters. Some early-morning riders had just come in – young girls, their mother, and a man. They talked of good cheap jodhpurs for the children and where one could get a green and brown check coat. One of the girls had evidently set her heart on this.

I did not want to feel at a disadvantage to the riders, but I did. They looked so clean and smart and trim. When I heard them asking each other what they would do for the rest of the day, I felt happier. I knew what I would do, but they seemed lost and bored, now that their ride was over.

I paid my bill and then walked through the town until I reached the moor again. I had decided to make for Dartmeet where there was another hostel. I did not love the moor, I thought, as I trudged along; it was too unrelieved and hostile, the colours were all torrid, smouldering purple, burnt orange-peel, dull green and ash colour.

At one point, just before I reached the hostel, I went down to the river and jumped from rock to rock until I reached the middle of the stream. No one was about; the silver water gushed over the stones in sparkling ribs. I pulled my clothes off hurriedly and slid in, holding on to the side of the rock with my hands. The current was swift; I crouched down and let the water race over me. It turned my skin to gooseflesh, making all the hairs erect on my body. I pulled myself out, shuddering; and rubbed my arms roughly with my dirty towel. I wanted to lie on the rock, quite naked, so that the sun should warm me through, but remembered that in this country one is arrested for that sort of thing.

Up I climbed to the hostel; my teeth chattered and my chest and arms still felt rough, like shagreen under my shirt. This hostel, like the last, was part of a farmhouse, but the whole scene was different; there was a gloomy, evil atmosphere of dirt and boredom. The meat-red walls of the outhouse, which served as a common-room, soared up into black dust-laden rafters. Over the green glass panes was a murky film of concretion. This one window let all the light in that there was.

I talked to the youngish farmer and his dogs – one had a blind eye, grey and opaque, like a boiled cod's eye. Then I wandered about in the nearby fields, not wanting to go back to the common-room.

When at last I did return, I found other arrivals. How pleased I was! I didn't care what they were like. I talked away the evening with a beefy man in a very white shirt and his smaller, quick-moving friend. It was all about food and distances, map-reading and the north of England. It was very nice and placid.

I walked to Princetown in the morning; I dawdled over the moor, only seeing it when my thoughts returned to me from far away. The

prison loomed up and brought back my attention to my surroundings; I had the sudden fancy that it was really a fortress, not a prison,
that the inmates would pour fire and molten lead out of those rows
of blind, unwinking windows if anyone attempted to go near them.

In the grey town, the first thing I noticed was a name-plate on a
door, stating that a warden or some official of the prison lived there.

I went down the main street; the prison had coloured all my
thoughts, and I saw the stone houses as grim faces with mouths shut
like traps. The upstairs windows were eyes, the chocolate-brown
doors the trap-like mouths.

I suddenly felt very hungry. I walked quickly to a shop and saw
with exaggerated delight that I was able to buy my favourite wheat
biscuit. I brought the sunset orange and red packet (so accurately
square) and some tenderized prunes.

Taking these with me across the street, I sat down with no more
ado at the foot of the war memorial and started to eat. A wave of
guilt spread over me as I munched with so much pleasure; the guilt
seemed even to add to my pleasure in some way. I thought of all the
prisoners in their cells, with their shaved heads and their canvas
clothes. I thought of the warder's eyes staring through the grating,
watching the furtive pleasure one might try to snatch, seeing the
little things that people do when they're alone, which it is so
shameful for other people to see. I thought of the dreadful food, the
offal in the stew, served in billy-cans. I saw the chaplain with damp
hand-clasp, bringing tattered novels. Then I heard all the convicts
battering on their doors, screaming and blaspheming half the night.

I got up, having at last filled myself with disquiet. I thought my
mental picture was probably twisted all awry, but whether it were
only novel-trash or not did not matter; the reality would be just as
horrible even though it were in a quite different way. The real
horrors and barbarities that were only able to grow between one
stupid man in power and one stupid man his victim. Horrors of petty
torture, such as are practised in private schools, only now with the
face uncovered, the white teeth showing.

From the prison I walked to the abbey. I wanted to see the monks
of Buckfast at work. I even played with the idea of giving myself up

to them and asking to be allowed to stay. I thought of the youth I'd
read of, who'd run away from the sea to go to them. This was an
inversion of the old adventure story that appealed to me. Now he
was quietly working, laying bricks or digging trenches. I thought
that I too was just the right age to surrender myself. I remembered
how as a schoolboy, when I'd seen the sandalled monks at Cowfold,
I'd had the same feeling of excitement, the desire to join them, to
see what it was like.

But when I thought clearly, I always realized that my idea of being
a monk was that I should have a stone cell in a garden with honey
bees buzzing close to me in an old rush-woven hive, and with enormous sunflowers nodding their black faces along my hedge; that I
should have a crystal crucifix and the loveliest old primitive that
money could extort from its original monastery; that I should have
a gushing spring and delicious food from heaven, and that in the
evenings when I wanted change and company I'd walk across the
fields to the abbey and sit talking half the night with other monks I
loved.

When I came to Buckfastleigh I did not even go to look at the
outside of the abbey. I knew I should not dare to go in. I have always
felt anxiety in the company of monks and nuns. To see them staring
at one through the grille in the gates of their monasteries is alarm-
ing. That inside world seems likely to trip one up and confuse one
at every turn.

I walked on to Dartington where I found the hostel housed in a
spotless cottage belonging to the Hall. I read about the school of
mime, the handicrafts, the agriculture, the children's school, the
ancient building itself. It all seemed so vital and interesting an experiment that I left straight away to find the Hall. When I got to the
gates, I found that I could not go in. A time was set for sightseers
earlier in the day. I looked along the huge expanse of gravel and saw
at the end what I imagined to be the banqueting hall. It looked
medieval, with buttresses.

Walking back along a wooded road I came upon a shop which
sold things made of wood and tweed materials. Without any
intention to buy I went up to it and looked around me. One could
tell how uncommercial the whole concern was. The building
was expensively simple and the woman who came out to me

just smiled rather ineffectually and pleasantly, then went away again.

This experiment in living excited me. Here were some rich people actually trying to construct something from their money.

Back at the hostel I tried to find out more about the place, but nobody could tell me much. There seemed to be no warden, only a woman who came in to clean every day.

The cottage was in a little hollow, and on the very edge of a stream. Already a mist was gathering over the water and blowing in at the windows. The walls outside and in were whitewashed and the floor was scrubbed concrete. The stoves were in perfect order and there was electric light.

I went in search of food for my evening meal. I was only able to buy porridge oats, and the shop man directed me to a farm where I could get cream.

I stood waiting at the door, and then the woman led me down to the stone dairy. The smell was a little revolting, and I did not like to see her breaking the thick yellow crust of the bowls of cream. It looked so like a scab on a wound, and broke in just that way.

I took my carton back with me and started to cook my oats. I had never made porridge before and I was afraid that it would be lumpy or burnt. I watched it with great care, stirring and smoothing it with my spoon until I thought it cooked.

Others who had arrived laughed at my care and told me that it was not breakfast time but supper.

After the meal we sat round the open window, which now was belching in the white mist, and talked. Nobody thought of shutting the window. The stream tinkled mournfully over the stones. I watched a spray of creeper waving against the dark sky, then decided to leave the others and go to bed.

They came in just as I was about to go to sleep. I heard them talking about waterproof capes, and telling dirty jokes. The jokes got more and more preposterous and led gradually to lustful imaginings and serious stories. Knitting the anecdotes together, binding the whole conversation, were the swear words; they were sprayed into every nook and cranny, to leave no void or empty space.

I woke once in the night, and saw the mist eddying about in the black room. Men snored gently; the grey square of light from the window seemed flat and opaque as a wooden hoarding.

By twelve o'clock the next morning I was at Thunderstone. Some people in a car had stopped and given me a lift. We hardly spoke as we sped along. At Kingsbridge I got out and thanked them. They smiled fat, animal smiles and sped on their way again.

I walked between two folds of hills, down to the little village. At the end of the stone breakwater, where it joined the rocks, I saw someone bathing. I walked out, gazing at the figure idly. He had pulled down his bathing-suit and was drying himself now. When I got to the end I saw, with a shock, that it was Green Anderson who had been at school with me. His flesh was just as green – yellow, sallow green – and his hair stood up in the same black, grass-like tufts. I remembered his jutting-out jaw and the rather atavistic sloping back of his low forehead. He looked up at me and then shouted, 'Good God, hullo Welch! Did you see me down on the beach?'

'No,' I answered, 'I didn't know it was you until I reached this spot.'

We talked quite animatedly while he dried, and pulled his clothes on. He jerked the towel over his golliwog's hair until it stood out in all directions.

'Come back and see my people,' he said.

We returned along the breakwater and I found that Mr and Mrs Anderson were two fat people sitting on the beach. There was a little too much dignity about them for their situation. They smiled at me and said, 'So you knew each other at Brook House.' They asked me where I was going to next and what I was training to be.

I wondered if they'd ask me to lunch, and if so, whether I should accept or refuse. I wondered what their lunch would be like.

When they clambered to their feet ponderously I decided that it was time to leave. I said good-bye, they all smiled, and we parted with no pain or pleasure.

Up on the hill stood a large hotel. I went into it and sat down self-consciously in the dining-room. The dreary family parties came in and looked at me as a stranger, then they smiled and went on with their cold meat and prunes and rice. The children seemed particularly unattractive. Life in this sort of seaside hotel is at its lowest ebb, I thought. Everyone's bored, even the slovenly waiters are bored. The food has no taste; and this afternoon people will lie on their beds and read novels, hoping in that way to shorten the interval before dinner.

I left the place as soon as possible and in walking up the hill outside I heard someone on a balcony say, 'How can anyone think that's pleasure? When I go on holiday I want to enjoy myself, not trudge like a tramp along a dusty road with a pack on my back.'

I looked up to see who had spoken that I should hear. I saw a youngish man whose fair hair was sparse and thin. He had well-covered arms and neck showing from his green sports shirt and he spoke to a girl who sat beside him.

I immediately hated him – his silly words, his voice, and his fleshy arms.

Is it to impress the woman, I thought angrily, that he pretends to be so mondaine – so 'sophisticated', as he would be sure to put it? That pitiful attempt at playing the bored man-about-town; didn't he know that it was soiled and tawdry when Horace Walpole was young? Didn't that fat cow's face know that the best thing for it would be to sweat away some of Windledon costiveness?

I was getting altogether too hot about the affair; but I have found that the one thing that enrages me is to overhear what I have been meant to overhear.

After his words I began suddenly to feel tired, to feel hot and dirty and dissatisfied. I walked wearily into Salcombe and thought of Tennyson. The sun on the water – Crossing the Bar; I wondered who had told me all about it. In the piled up and seemingly terraced town I saw someone painting in a picturesque nook. An open door, a geranium in a window, the harbour seen through a narrow crack between the houses, they were all there.

I left the town and crossed the bar myself.

From here again my journey is lost. I only know that I spent one night in a hostel perched on the side of a steep hill with trees all round it, and that I found a silver spoon there. It seemed to be sent specially to compensate me for the one I'd lost at Midhurst. This was a modern spoon, but thick, and with a rounded end. I put it in my rucksack with satisfaction, wondering who had left it.

Further on my journey I know I walked with a boy from Bermondsey. He was full of gaiety and content, telling me all about his office work, his delight in the country.

'Why don't you get a business job,' he kept on asking me, 'and make some money? Art's no good for making money.' Then he would stop and bubble over with pleasure at the wood we were walking through, or the view from the hill top.

'Bloody lovely,' he'd say; 'it's bloody lovely,' or 'Christ, what a place this is! It's fucking wonderful.' I was delighted with so much exuberance and listened to him carefully, for he swore and shouted his praise with so much fervour that his sentences were really startling.

We seemed to run and skip a great deal of the way. He was always chasing something and getting me to follow, leaping streams and fences.

Once when we bathed in a rocky pool I saw the ingrained dirt in his white back – little black spots like pepper across the skin.

'Scratch it,' he said urgently, offering it to me and arching it like an animal's, 'it itches like hell, Christ how it itches!' I scratched with my nails until he gave contented guttural noises. I left long red lines on the white skin in a strange criss-cross pattern. 'Now you look tattooed,' I shouted, 'you don't know what I've written on your back!'

He came to duck me and I floundered away from him into the trees.

With the sunlight dappling our skin, we raced in and out of the trees until he knocked me down and sat on me. I felt the twigs digging into my back.

'Get off,' I yelled, 'you're suffocating me.' He rolled down beside me and we lay there till the sun had dried us.

I must have lost him soon after this, for he was not with me when I entered Taunton.

It was evening, and I found that I only had a few shillings left in my pocket; meals in hotels and other small extravagances had done their work. I knew that on the next day I would have to think seriously. I put it off till then, refusing to look at the problem.

I found the hostel in the High Street quite full. People walked about with cooking pots in their hands, whistling or singing as they made their evening meal. One couple I particularly noticed, chiefly because other people also were giving them covert glances.

The man was in very short corduroy shorts and a dirty coral shirt. His hairy legs were bare and he had a curly, brown, rather matted beard. On his feet were sandals made only of thin straps of dried and cracking leather. He wore a ring of lapis and a cross on a greasy string round his neck.

The girl was perhaps less startling; she was plump with wide hips also encased in green corduroy. Her hair was a natural brassy colour, worn resting on the shoulders, and her make-up seemed to consist of oatmeal, cochineal and coffee. I don't know why the kitchen ingredients jumped into my mind, but I know that her cosmetics did remind me of food; perhaps it was because they were applied with the same sort of carelessness as cooks have when they mix their dishes.

The man looked at me as he passed; he was carrying a sausage on a fork.

'Good evening,' he said, in one of those sweet soft voices which are so affected that it is difficult to tell the speaker's place of origin. This voice might have been anything; it sounded cockney, cultured, Welsh, French to me.

After he and his girl had eaten their sausages, he came over to talk to me, leaving her to do the washing-up.

'Ah, I thought you were an artist too,' he said, having questioned me and found that I was at an art school. 'I never went to an art school myself, I think they're inventions of the devil; I just started painting on my own in a studio over a shop.'

Hearing more of his voice, I now realized that he was English and that all the strangeness of his tones was due to conscious effort. I looked at his face more closely. It was good-looking and unattractive as bearded faces often are. He had those thin, delicately-made features which I do not like, perhaps because I share the conventional association of them with coldness and cruelty.

He went on talking to me, telling me how he ran across the road to fetch his meals from a little restaurant, if he could not be bothered to cook them; otherwise he cooked his kippers and his sausages on the gas-ring in the studio. The girl, I gathered, was often there to help him or pose for him. She sat and mended his clothes for him too, but they did not live together.

'And do you manage to sell your pictures?' I asked, trying to make this difficult question sound polite.

'Yes,' came his light, surprising answer, 'I manage to get rid of them very well. I know most people moan and groan that nobody buys anything nowadays, but I don't find any difficulty. Whenever I want any more money I just take a picture round to a little man I know and he sells it for me.'

This was all said in a vague, distant, casual tone that somehow failed to be convincing. It was the exaggerated casualness, I think, rather than the preposterous story, which made one disbelieve.

Everything about this person seemed a caricature, an over-drawing of some novel character. I wondered how he had managed to make and preserve the businessman, and to poke fun at the dreary money-grabber; he fitted perfectly into a very worn-out pattern.

'Ma chère,' he called out, 'ma chère, come over here and talk with us.'

The girl came and sat down stolidly beside him. He stroked her hair and hummed a little song; then he smiled sweetly and withdrew into a deep reverie.

It was interesting to me to see someone so overlaid as this. Such consistency was very unusual.

It seemed unnatural to me to see the man and the woman separated that night. This did not fit in with the picture of the gas-ring, the kippers, the dirt between the toes and the immortal canvases.

When I saw them in the morning, going off on a battered green tandem, pedalling soberly, I again had the feeling that this was a little out of keeping with his carefully built-up character. Surely they should have travelled with a donkey or a dear little goat in harness.

I walked into the streets of Taunton, not knowing what I was going to do. To write or telegraph to my aunt for money would take too long; besides, I did not like to think of her face when she received the notice. She did not have charge of my money affairs now and she would consider my request a great nuisance and just like me. If I wrote to my father's office it would take even longer and there would be even more questions to answer.

I decided to do neither of these things, but to walk in the direction of home until something happened. This was really not a decision at all, but simply the *absence* of any plan.

As I walked along the main road cars shot past me, making me envious of their speed. I was just beginning to wonder if I should ever be offered a lift when a rather disreputable car passed me, slowed down, and finally stopped. The driver was looking back, craning his neck out of the window.

'Want a lift?' he yelled heartily.

I ran forward, feeling very grateful. I fitted myself into the seat beside him and slammed the door, making it shake crazily.

'How far do you want to go?' my companion asked. He wore a Harris tweed cap which matched his tawny little moustache, and his face was thin and smooth and pink.

'As far as I can; I've run out of money and I've got to get home.' I laughed, feeling the next moment I should not have mentioned my penniless state to a stranger.

He smiled, looking straight in front of him.

'Well, I can take you as far as Stonehenge. Is that any good to you? After that I've got to branch off.'

'Oh, that'll be marvellous,' I said, 'it seems half across England when you're walking; it must be sixty or seventy miles at least.'

The rattling car was speeding along now. The man began to speak to me as if he'd known me for a long time. He asked me, not too obtrusively, where I'd been to school, and told me that he had been at Charterhouse.

'And what do you do now?' he asked.

'I'm at an art school.'

'Oh, that's interesting, because I work for a firm of cloth manufacturers and we badly want some new designs for shirt materials. Do you think that would be in your line at all? We want some new stripes and smart designs to compete with the French, who at present produce all the best "English" shirt materials. Rather odd, isn't it?' he laughed.

I was surprised at this sudden proposal. He seemed quite serious.

'I've only done designs for curtain fabrics,' I said, 'big patterns to be printed by hand from wood-blocks. How does one set about designing for machine printing? I suppose the thing to do is to make a very accurate drawing on paper?'

I secretly wished that this subject had not arisen; I did not care for the idea of designing shirt stripes. It seemed such very paltry, insignificant work. 'What is there to design?' I thought. 'A stripe is a stripe.'

We went on talking for some time about the intricacies of shirt stripes, and I promised to do some designs and send them to him, if I had the time. I added this to exonerate me, for I knew that I would never think of designing a shirt stripe. This is what people call 'missing an opportunity' I thought, and I wished that one day someone might offer me an opportunity which I would want to take.

Racing along in the car, I saw nothing. I listened to my new friend and at the same time became conscious of a curious smell growing ever stronger as the heat of the day increased. It came from the back of the car and reminded me of cheese, wine and fish glue – a really terrible smell. It had such body and strength that it seemed to coat the insides of my nostrils, clinging there in a layer.

Once I looked round swiftly and saw nothing but piles of cardboard boxes and some luggage.

'Is it the dressing on the shirts,' I asked myself, 'or does he travel in cheeses also?'

He was soon telling me anecdotes of sport and amusement abroad. He knew the South of France and Austria. Except for the extraordinary smell the atmosphere was urbane, not to say fashionable. I liked him, for he was kind and tolerant, accepting everything as it was.

'What's the time?' he said, looking at his wrist. 'It's after one, we'd better stop and have something to eat.'

This was a moment of embarrassment for me, for I had hardly any food in my rucksack and I knew that he would insist on my sharing some of his own provisions.

He stopped the car and leant over the back of the seat, dragging at one of the suitcases. He pulled it out and suggested that we should have our meal in the fields. Leaving the car on the side of the road, we went through a gate which led us into a little green glade, surrounded by trees. We sat down on his mackintosh and he opened the suitcase.

It contained nothing but a huge Dundee cake and several bottles of cider.

'Have a piece,' he said, cutting a thick, flat chunk for me and holding it out.

I took it, protesting that I ought not to eat his food.

'Don't be absurd, look at the size of the cake,' he said. It was, indeed, enormous.

He chucked one of the bottles of cider over to me recklessly.

'Wash it down with that,' he ordered. The bottle fizzed and buzzed at being treated so roughly.

I murmured another remark, and opened the bottle. Tiny bubbles rose to the neck and made a slight foam there. I tilted it to my lips and swallowed the foam and the red-gold liquid; then I bit into the rich cake.

The sun was beating down now, making the grass humid and dank, almost drawing steam from it. The elms in the fields by the road were heavy and grey with dust.

My companion began to tell me sexy stories. He did it with the bored, well-bred manner people often assume for these occasions.

'. . . and that was that,' he drawled, giving me only the shadow of a smile at the end.

We were eating a great deal of the cake, and two bottles lay empty in the grass.

He opened another for me and held it out. I took it, feeling rather dazed; my head had begun to buzz and the heavy cake seemed to be ploughing about inside me.

When we got up to go I felt quite drunk, chiefly, I think, on account of the sun beating down on my head as I drank the two large bottles of fizzy cider.

I was ashamed to disclose my weak head to my companion, so after we had both turned our faces to the bushes, I carefully allowed him to lead the way back to the car.

I wedged myself in to the deflated tub seat and we rattled off again. I leant with my face to the window, hoping that the wind would revive me. I hoped never to see plum cake again in my life.

He left me exactly at the fork where Stonehenge stands.

'Good-bye,' he said, 'don't forget about the designs.'

I was already half-thinking of the monoliths.

'Good-bye, thank you so much. I can hardly believe I've come so far in one day. You've no idea how it's helped me.' I waved to him and watched him disappearing with his cheese smell and those mysterious cardboard boxes.

I went quickly round the wire enclosure to the entrance where I paid my sixpence. It ought to be all alone on the open plain, I thought, not enclosed in wire and caught in the fork of two main roads.

The little man in the wooden booth looked sour and disgruntled. He clipped off my ticket and I was inside the enclosure.

As I walked quickly towards the stones, I caught up a woman and her daughter; at least I supposed they were mother and daughter, they seemed so to me, for one was middle-aged and one was young, and both had small heads and short, clipped, mannish hair.

'Oh, isn't it wonderful?' the young girl said to me. 'I've come thousands of miles to see this and it's worth it.'

The mother turned round and seemed to accept me in a moment. She smiled but said nothing. They both wore sandals and short kilted skirts. The girl had slung across her shoulder a very efficient-looking little German camera.

'We've just come from London where we thought the parks were so lovely,' the girl went on. 'In America we've got nothing like that. You can't imagine how different it is.'

She stood on a fallen stone which slanted into the earth. Looking down at her feet, she described more of the wonders of England and the emptiness of America. Her quiet voice seemed almost despairing Everything was new to her; she gave praise and blame, as if it were a duty. She gave me to understand in a moment that they were poor and that they loved culture and beauty better than anything else in the world.

I left them still standing on the stone, in the middle of Salisbury Plain.

Now that I was so much nearer home I could spend my few remaining shillings with a more comfortable feeling. I spent that night at the Nether Wallop Hostel and the next day moved on to Winchester. The warden remembered me and seemed pleased to see me; I thought that if necessary I would ask her to lend me the money for my train fare back to Sussex, but first I wanted to see a little more of Winchester and its surroundings.

That afternoon I spent looking at the antique shops. There was a sort of covered-in mart, piled high with furniture, only narrow alleys being left between. Perched dangerously on its tables were pieces of china and plate – cheese covers, egg-cup stands and tobacco jars. I found two royal blue and gold saucers and a cup marked with tiny crescents on the bottom. The blue and gold husks hung in swags from gold medallions and underneath all this decoration the china was fluted.

I took the Worcester pieces to the shopman and asked him, 'How much?' He said, 'Half-a-crown,' and I, thinking of my almost empty pocket, said, 'One-and-six.' I won, after a little more arguing, and took the things away delightedly. They proved to be a great nuisance and anxiety at the hostel, as I was for ever wondering if someone had knocked them from the rickety shelf beside my bed. At last I gave them to the warden to keep.

As I bathed in the river under the mill the next morning, I thought that I would walk all that day up the banks of the Itchen, exploring for as far as I could go.

I climbed out of the town up a narrow rather slum-like street, and at one point, on looking back, I saw the enormous squat cathedral crouching to the ground like an animal. The smooth roofs dominated and half-hid the walls and buttresses. I saw the cross-shape clearly.

I kept as near to the river as possible, walking for most of the time through rich fields. Once I had to leave the path, for I came out near a house and a woman appeared, saying, 'You can't come by here, this is a gentleman's residence.'

'Isn't there a footpath?' I asked as pleasantly as possible.

'No, there is not.' She didn't smile back; she seemed outraged that I should think of appearing in the grounds of a gentleman's residence. Was she the cook, or the housekeeper, or perhaps even the gentleman's wife? I shall never know.

I reached the river again on the other side of the house; and here it looked enticing, so wonderfully clear that I could see every stone and weed on its bed. I could resist it no longer. I sat down in the deep grass and pulled my shirt and trousers off; then I crawled to the crumbling bank and let myself down into the crystal water. It was too shallow to swim; I just sat on the bottom and held my arms out. The gentle current swayed me about like a weed. I felt myself lifted and then set down again gently on the pebbles.

I kept so still that large prune-velvet fish sailed in the water near me. They only moved their fins now and then, to keep their dead

straight position; otherwise they made no progress forwards or back-
wards, but only worked their gills and looked disillusioned.

When the water began to chill me through, I crawled out and lay
in the grass with the sun beating down on me. My eyes were closed,
so I did not see the little boy until he stood over me. His nose was dribbling, making a little channel through the dirt on his face, and he wore
braces over his ragged shirt. His eyes had gone round with surprise.

'You been bathing?' he asked. I nodded my head.

'Coo, you'll cop it, you'll cop it,' he crowed with delight, 'nobody
can't bathe in that river, it's private and kept for the fish. You'll cop
it, you'll cop it.' He danced round me waving the stick he'd been
peeling.

I sat up and started to pull on my shirt. I saw the little boy staring
at me and realized that he was curious about my grown-up body. I
remembered, when I'd first gone to see my father in his bath, how
surprised I was. At home, I thought, this little boy has never seen his
father or his elder brothers naked; they probably just wash their
chests and arms and bundle into bed at night.

I had now pulled on my trousers, and stood up. If the little boy
was right, and I saw that he was, I must not stay to be caught by some
officious person. The thing I hate most is to be insulted by some
repulsive stranger.

'Don't you ever bathe here?' I asked. 'It's lovely.'

'Nevoow!' he made the short word into a long one. 'I tell you, it's
private for the fish. They'll lock you up if they catch you.'

And again, at the prospect of my being taken to prison, he danced
and jumped about, bending his stick until he broke it.

'Good-bye,' I said, walking away.

'Good-bye,' he brought out with a jerk. He was still staring at me
and scowling, trying to make me out.

I left the river banks and walked towards Old Alresford.

Passing through the wide, silent main street I came to a red
Georgian house and watercress beds lying below it on the other side
of the road. I looked down on to the stone-green plants growing in
their accurate, terraced squares. The jagged shapes of water, seen
between the dark leaves, glistened like silver oil on a road at night.

Further on I came to a ruined petrol pump outside a wooden hut.
A huge yellow enamel hoarding for motor tyres straddled a ditch to

one side. The boys and men had flung stones at it; it was pock-marked all over with rusty splintered stars.

I seemed to be coming to a forgotten part; the bare fields stretched away on either side of me and there was only one cottage in view. As I passed, I pictured it as housing several small orphans and illegitimates. I saw them in egg-and-dribble-dirty bibs playing with the refuse at the back of the house. And I saw the huge-bosomed baby-farmer, her chapped red hands glowing against her grease-stiff apron.

I so believed in my own story that now, when I look back, I see a notice outside the cottage to say that it is a branch of a certain orphanage where young children are sent 'to have the country air'. An indescribable threat seems to lie, for me, in those last five words.

I left the grim cottage behind, but still took with me imaginings of beatings in the lamplight. I saw the baby-farmer's husband coming in from work at night, tired and filthy. He unbuckles his thick belt and strips it off in exasperation. Then all the air is filled with scream-ing as he beats the boy's tender flesh till it is broken. I hear all the other children crying with the boy and see rods in the corner of the kitchen sticky with blood.

But surely that is rather a worn-out picture of a baby-farm, I told myself, to clear away the image.

The telegraph wires hummed and moaned; there were no more houses, only fields of poor-looking grass bending down under the wind.

At last I saw a farm track slanting across a field and leading to some buildings. I saw the little sign at the gate, Y.H.A., and turned in thankfully.

As I drew nearer I saw that the building nearest to me was of stone and that it had lancet windows; behind it stood the brick farm-house. My excitement grew, I wanted to know about the ancient part. I wondered if I should sleep in it.

A woman met me at the wicket gate, close to the round duck-pond. She wore a brown wool dress and her eyes seemed out of focus. 'Good evening,' she said, smiling at me vaguely. 'You coming to the hostel?'

'Yes,' I answered, 'and can you tell me what this part is which looks so like a chapel.'

'That *is* the hostel, but it used to be, centuries ago, a chapel and a place of rest for travellers which the Knights Hospitaller set up. A priest lived there, sleeping in the upstairs room. Downstairs is a kitchen eating room and the chapel, which is now turned into the common-room. Come in and see it.'

She led me through a low gothic door into what had been the chapel. It had perfect lancet windows on each side, but the east window had been blocked and an ugly inglenook fireplace built against it.

'Did the Hostel Association do that?' I asked, pointing at the fireplace.

'Yes, they built the chimney, but the window had been blocked for years. You can see outside a few fragments of tracery built into the wall. It must have been done long, long ago, the stone is all the same colour and covered with lichen.' She called it 'litchen.'

'You see, this chapel and whole building has been used as a barn and storing place by the farm until last year when I let the Y.H.A. convert it. That's why it's so untouched I think, because, ever since the Knights Hospitaller left, it's only been used as an outhouse.'

She took me into the kitchen part. It was a low small room with a spiral stone staircase leading from it. The whole scene seemed to smell of a medieval hermit to me. I was halfway up the stairs before she'd begun to climb them.

'You're in a hurry,' she said.

'Oh, yes, I want to see everything; I've never before come across a little medieval house like this. It's exactly what I've always wanted for myself. Why, it's got everything! Kitchen, chapel, living-room, bedroom . . .'

'And privy!' she added to my list with a naughty twinkle.

'Where? Where's the gothic privy?' I asked, looking round me. I was all agog to see the gothic privy.

'There,' she said, pointing to a little door at the entrance of the bedroom.

I opened it and there was a little closet with shaped stone seat and a shaft cutting right down in the wall of the building and then deep into the ground.

'Didn't they construct them beautifully!' I said, looking at the carved seat and the tiny trefoil window which gave one so charming a view of the pond and the fields. And suddenly, as I looked at the shaft, I realized what the 'garde-robe' had been in the Priory at Repton.

In one corner of the upstairs landing had been a little nook labelled, 'Prior's garde-robe'; there was a small trap door on the new oak floor and when one opened it a stone shaft, very like this one, was discovered. Because the stone seat above had disappeared I had never understood this hole. I remembered one afternoon investigating the hole and asking other people what they thought it could be. We all decided that the nook was where the Prior kept his clothes, 'garde-robe' reminding us of ward-robe, but the shaft we could not understand.

Now I knew. I turned to the woman and saw her looking at me anxiously.

'It's never to be used, you know,' she said firmly, 'the proper lavatory is over at the farm.'

'But of course not!' I agreed. 'One can't use a medieval privy; such a relic is almost sacred. Besides, we have no sand and spices and sweet smells to throw down afterwards. I'm sure they did all that, aren't you? We've no idea of their refinements, because we don't think on the same lines. We make all these arrangements practical and rather sordid; whereas they tried to spiritualize them a little. It's the same with food; we don't like spices and herbs, but they did because they gave the ordinary meat a sort of glamour.'

I now began to look round the bedroom. On one side of the arched stone fireplace was a squint-hole. I went up to it and looked down into the chapel.

'That's so that the priest could keep an eye on the pilgrims and travellers,' the farmer said, for she herself *was* the farmer, as I learnt afterwards.

There was only one lancet window; the opening broadened out, as it cut through the thickness of the wall, in the way that delighted me so when, as a child, I was taken to see castles.

All round the walls were double-decker iron beds with red blankets.

'Do you think I'll sleep here all alone tonight?' I asked the woman, with an exaggerated shudder.

'I expect so, unless anyone turns up late, which is unlikely.' And at once she began with relish to tell me of a figure which had been seen limping round the old Knights Hospitallers' chapel.

'We think it must be the ghost of one of the old priests in charge, for we found a skeleton buried outside the east end, just under the window. It had a deformed leg-bone. I know,' she said severely, 'because I am a trained nurse. Anyone with a bone like that in his leg would have most certainly limped.'

She said all this with a far-away smile, as if she were thinking more of the effect her words would produce than the truth. I felt that she was romancing and elaborating but wanted to hear more.

'What did you do with the bones after you'd dug them up?' I asked, wanting to see this deformed bone.

'We buried them again, of course,' she said, repressively and piously.

'Have you seen the lame priest yourself?' I insisted.

'No, I don't think so, unless I once caught a glimpse of him, just turning the corner of the spiral staircase.'

Now I knew that she was fabricating, but I did not mind; she seemed a lively person, still wanting to amuse herself with life.

'Come into the house and sign the book,' she said, leading me across the yard. 'But I must warn you that I have a patient with me who is recovering from a nervous breakdown. Although I've owned this farm now for sixteen years I still have convalescent cases sent to me by my old patients and colleagues in hospital.'

She took me into the farm dining-room, and although it was a large room it seemed difficult to move in it because of the huge Victorian walnut sideboard and table. The furniture designer must have been inspired by the Jacobean, I think, for all the legs were twisted into spirals, and large heraldic beasts held up virgin shields on the crests of the chairs and above the sideboard. Frothy ferns and large pieces of plate decorated the tops of the furniture.

Through all this I saw a pale man with a rug across his shoulders sitting by the empty grate. He got up, when we came in, and looked about him anxiously. He seemed almost about to throw himself out of the window into the garden.

The farmer introduced me to him as 'one of our young walkers come to spend the night in the Chapel of Ease.'

After this announcement the man became so nervous that he held his thin hand out to me, then withdrew it, thrust it out again, and, after giving me one desperate look, flung out of the room, shutting the door behind him with surprising stealthy quietness.

'Oh, he puts it all on,' the farmer said exasperatedly. 'I know nervous cases, I've nursed hundreds of them. He should be perfectly all right by now. He just wants everyone to know how ill he's been. Now he'll go wandering about all over the fields and I'll have to fetch him in when it gets dark. He's all right with me. I can always soothe him down.'

She held out the book to me and showed me where to sign. As I was bending over it, one of her daughters came in. I looked up and saw a plump girl staring at me. She was a year or two younger than I was and she wore a very sleek, self-satisfied air.

'This is Myrna,' her mother said, putting an arm round her waist. The girl put the arm away from her as if it had been a log of wood, bobbed her head to me in a perfunctory little nod and went out again without saying anything.

'You wouldn't think she's shy, but she is,' her mother said.

I went out through the kitchen, and in the porch at the back door I saw a cat teaching her kittens to play with a mouse. The mouse was not yet dead and a thrill of horror ran through me as I saw it squirm under the paw of one of the little fluffy kittens. They did not bite it or even let their claws out to it; they just stared at it with their large blue eyes and patted it every now and then playfully as they would a ball of wool. The mother sat upright, watching, taking no part unless the mouse tried to escape; then she would reach out her long paw and cuff it viciously until it seemed to lie dead.

'Won't you kill it, or take it away?' I asked the woman urgently.

'Good Lord, no,' she smiled, 'they're learning to be good mousers. How do you think she can teach them if we interfere?'

I hurried away, not being able to watch any longer, and started to make my evening meal. The farmer had sold me eggs and I had tomatoes.

The pink mess in the saucepan was too liquid, but I ate it with a spoon and it was good.

After exploring the building again I sat down in the chapel, wondering what to do. I looked up at the three remaining curved beams in the roof; they made the newer straight ones look thin and cheap. I fell to thinking of the chapel as I would restore it. I saw the east window opened once again, the ugly inglenook taken away, the roof restored so that all the beams should be like the three heavy shaped ones.

I was woken from these imaginings by the opening of the heavy gothic door; a large man and a small woman stepped down into the room. Both wore rucksacks which they slipped off their shoulders with signs of relief.

'We've got here at last!' the girl said. 'We thought we'd never find it.'

'Have you come far?' I asked, getting up.

'All through the most marvellous woods,' the man answered. 'You've no idea. What a day we've had! This is the country for me.'

The girl was looking at him anxiously, holding one of his fingers and twining hers round and round it.

'Ducky,' she almost whined, 'we must get our supper on. Will you go and ask the lady for eggs and milk?'

As soon as he left she said to me, 'This looks a very interesting old place. After we've got a bit of something inside us, we'll want to go exploring.' She gave a genteel little laugh and started to unpack the rucksacks. Dark curls fell over her face, and her hands darted about rapidly. I saw that she was a very efficient little woman.

He came back holding several eggs in one of his large hands. From the other dangled a bottle of milk, against the deep blue of his rugger shorts. The shorts, cut on the curve, almost with wings, looked strange and exotic in the chapel; but I could tell, when I looked at him more closely, that he was just the person to play that game well. He had a little head, a little moustache, very broad shoulders, and a soft pink mouth never quite shut.

'Here you are, darling,' he said, holding the eggs and milk out to her.

'Oh, Dan, do be careful or you'll break the eggs in your clumsy way! Take them into the kitchen; I'm just screwing up the frying-pan handle.'

She finished tightening the collapsible handle. I saw that they had a very neat little nest of travelling utensils.

'There are some cooking pots in there,' I said, 'but perhaps you like to use your own. They look very nice ones.'

'Well, yes, we do, then you can be certain they're clean, can't you!' She gave me a vivacious smile and bustled into the kitchen carrying the rest of their provisions.

I heard her giving directions, and once or twice scolding him for clumsiness or laziness. I imagined him passing her wooden spoons, or cutting bread and becoming rather dazed by her quickness.

They came back into the chapel, bearing plates of fried tomatoes and eggs, and great mugs of steaming tea. The girl had fried golden door-steps of bread to go under the eggs and tomatoes.

'That's what I had too,' I said, 'only mine didn't look nearly so professional. I just mixed my eggs and tomatoes in a saucepan until I had a pink mess.'

They both laughed. The man said, 'Pink stuff, stink puff,' and transported me to St Michael's when I was eleven years old, and all the other boys said, 'Pink stuff, stink puff,' all day long.

The couple ate hungrily and almost in silence. The girl turned to him once and said, 'Do you like it, dear?' He nodded, with his mouth full, then got out, 'Darling, it's first rate.'

When the meal was over the man pushed his plate away and leant down to reach the pipe stuck in the top of his sock. As he knocked it out in the open fireplace an idea seemed to come to him.

'I say, shall we light the fire?' he suggested, turning to his girl and me.

'Oh, do you think we ought to?' she asked cautiously.

'Why not? The branches are already laid there, and it's chilly now the sun's gone down.'

The stone chapel with its high roof was indeed getting cold. Shadows had rounded off all the corners, and a black gloom floated above us in the rafters.

'Yes, let's light it,' I said, 'it'll keep the ghosts away.'

'Oogh, are there ghosts?' the girl asked, making herself shudder all over.

The man put his arm round her. 'Don't be silly, Vi,' he said, 'he's only teasing.'

Vi snuggled up to him, and for a moment I thought they were going to forget about me and the fire; then the girl broke from him, pushed back some of her curls, and said, 'We must put some more paper under the wood.'

She was down on her knees in a moment, crushing sheets of paper into balls and stuffing them under the branches. She held out her hand impatiently to Dan for the matches. Then she lit the pile in three places, and soon blue smoke spiralled up the chimney. Some of it came out into the room; but when the flames began to lick round the wood, the smoke subsided.

We sat back in our chairs and watched the fire.

'That's more like!' the man Dan said. Vi went to sit on the arm of his chair, then she sank down lower and lower, until they were lying beside each other on the dirty brown corduroy cushions. He reached round her to light his pipe, crossing his eyes as he looked at the bowl.

Now she lay with her head against his heart. He had thrown his head back and was blowing smoke up into the darkness of the ceiling.

'It's like sailing on the sea,' she said dreamily, and I did not quite know what she meant until I realized that she was talking of the rise and fall of his breathing.

He inflated his chest, then let the air gush out of his mouth suddenly. 'Now there's a stiff groundswell,' he said, doing it again.

Vi laughed and giggled, pretended to bite his nipple; she even put one of her hands between the buttons of his white shirt. He lay back, allowing her to do what she liked, contenting himself by only holding her against him.

The leaping fire gained strength; it ate the twigs up greedily, making them spit and sizzle and curl. Now it was flickering on the white walls, throwing up the carved shapes of the lancets, and covering with an apricot glow the bare arms and legs of the lovers.

They lay still for some time, until I thought that they might have fallen asleep, but at that moment the girl sat up, ready to tell me all about herself and Dan.

Dan was a medical student in the Midlands and she lived and worked nearby. They always tried to get their holidays together; then they went for these wonderful rambles in the country and returned home fit and brown and bursting with health.

They both used the word 'fit' several times.

'And may we ask what you do?' the man said to me.

'I'm an art student,' I said nervously.

'What else are you interested in?' he asked.

'Oh, I don't know – history, houses and the old things inside them.'

'But aren't you interested in Nature?' he asked incredulously. 'Do you mean to say you like old chairs and tapestry better than woods such as we've been in today? Surely there's nothing as beautiful as Nature! A fortnight like this keeps me going for the rest of the year.'

'I'm more interested in things made by human beings than I am in nature, but that doesn't mean that I don't like to walk in the country, else I wouldn't be here, would I?'

'But you probably only do it to get from one old ruin to another,' he said vehemently.

I hated all this nature-talk. It always brings the very worst out in people. I was silent until the girl said, 'We went to see the College at Winchester.'

The man turned to me.

'I don't know what school you went to,' he said, 'but my school, although you've probably never heard of it, was much larger than Winchester – why, there were eight hundred boys or more! It's queer how small some of these well-known schools are, isn't it?'

'I saw rather a sissy boy,' said Vi, rubbing her face against Dan's as she spoke.

'He only had a little white singlet on, and grey knickers, and he was running like anything, and his fair hair was all stuck to his face with perspiration. He was ever so thin and delicate-looking, I felt quite sorry for him.'

She pulled Dan's nose as she said this last sentence, hoping that he'd pretend to be jealous.

'Vi always seems to like "wets" so much; I often wonder why she ever took to me,' he said placidly.

'How do you know that I don't think you're a great big baby too?' she asked; and she wiped his face, as if pretending that he'd been dribbling.

'Oh, I say!' he fended her off aggrievedly. 'You'd better go after your Winchester boy if you want someone like that.'

For a few moments no one spoke; the other two were content to lie together in the chair, and I was embarrassed by the talk of 'wets', and the playful nose-pulling. Then the man turned to me and asked:

'How old are you?'

'Eighteen,' I said.

'Well, you look about sixteen, but you talk as if you were ten years older. I've never met anyone like that before; it's queer.'

'Yes, I couldn't quite make you out,' the girl chimed in, 'you seemed so young in some ways and quite grown-up in others.'

I sat back, confused, wondering what they would say next. It was difficult to tell whether they were paying me compliments or merely dissecting and analysing me to my face.

'Well, we're very pleased we found you here; it's good to have an interesting talk, isn't it, Vi?' She nodded her head. 'Yes, it's nice to have a discussion after a lovely day in the open air.'

For one moment more they lay back; then the girl said:

'Dan darling, I suppose we've got to go to bed. What a pity! I've got to go all across that dark stable-yard to the farmhouse. You must see me to the door; I couldn't go alone in the dark.'

He tried to struggle out of the chair, but they were too tightly wedged.

'Get up, you fat lump you!' he blustered, pretending to punch her sides. 'You may look small, Vi, but you're as fat as butter.'

'Oh, you are a brute to insult me so,' she wailed. She put her arms round his neck and seemed to flatten her face against his. I imagined mouths, noses, eyebrows pressed tightly together. I thought of their eyelashes tickling each other's cheeks, when their eyes blinked.

Vi jumped up, business-like and efficient again in a moment. She held her hand out to me. 'Good-night,' she said, 'this has been a nice evening. We'll see you in the morning, I hope.' Then she went out of the gothic door on Dan's arm. I heard her giving him instructions about the food and the bedding, as they crossed the yard. Once her voice seemed to be raised in protest. I could tell that she was managing, persuading and ordering him to do things.

'Darling, what's the good of doing anything unless you do it properly?' floated in at the open door.

He came back looking rather morose and cowed. We lit two candles and climbed up the spiral staircase. Our huge shadows were thrown on the curving wall.

'Now is the ghostly time, don't you think?' I said, to start him talking.

'The big shadows make it nice and creepy, don't they,' he answered.

He chose a bed opposite to mine and unrolled the red blankets; then he sat down and pulled off his shoes, his socks and his shorts. His pipe rattled out on to the floor and he bent forward anxiously, to retrieve it. 'Not broken, thank God,' he said.

He stuck it in his mouth, picked up his candle and started to wander round the room exploring. He looked grotesque with his bare legs and thighs, and with the pipe jutting out of his mouth. Putting his hands under his shirt, he beat a tattoo on his stomach.

I showed him the beautiful privy and he laughed. Then we both rolled into bed and blew out our candles.

'Glad there's no one up top to lean out and be sick,' he said. His double-decker bed swayed and creaked. 'God, don't they make a noise! You have to lie pretty still in this sort of bed! They remind you of a ship though, don't they.'

I agreed, and then we spoke no more. Soon he was breathing very deeply and once I heard him mutter a few words in his sleep. I lay awake for some time; when I opened my eyes I saw the faint, pointed shape of light from the one lancet window.

Vi came over from the farmhouse in the morning looking strained and anxious. She had been planning the whole day, and was terrified that Dan or some unseen force would spoil the pattern.

'Darling, do hurry up and help me with the breakfast, else we'll never get off; we're missing half the day!' she complained.

Dan lumbered about, stuffing things into rucksacks and then taking them out again hurriedly, before she ordered him to do so.

'What will it be like if they get married?' I thought. 'Will it all change? Will she become placid and cow-like and will he do the ranting and raving?'

I left them snatching mouthfuls of food between kissings and cursings and grumblings. Dan had begun to look rather truculent, and he kissed her dutifully.

I walked across to the farmhouse to pay my shilling for the night. The little mouse now lay dead in the kitchen porch. Neither the cat nor the kittens had eaten it; they paid no more attention, now that it could no longer run or scream. I found the nervous-breakdown man sitting by the empty grate in the dining-room as before. This time he did not make his escape, but contented himself by giving me a sort of skeleton grin; his mouth flashed into a fierce, square opening and remained thus for some moments.

The lady of the manor — she had already told me that the farm should be called the manor — gave me a sweet gracious smile and asked me if, before I left, I'd like to go and see the cows being milked. She herself led me through the mud past the round pond.

'That, of course, was the Knights Hospitallers' fish-pond,' she said, throwing out her hand gracefully. 'I expect they kept carp in it; there may even be some in it still. They live for hundreds of years, you know.'

She looked at me closely to see if I believed her.

'You didn't see the lame priest last night, did you? I expect you were glad for the company when those others arrived so late,' she added.

We walked a few more steps through the mud. Then she said:

'Just near here is the Tichborne estate. Have you ever heard of the Tichborne Claimant? I remember my father telling me that he saw the great fat butcher once.'

'I've read about it, and seen a print of the Claimant in court. It was hanging up in an old pub in Kent,' I answered. 'Mustn't it have been an amazing case!'

She left me at the milking-shed, saying, 'Ted will show you everything.'

Ted was pouring milk into the top of the cooler and letting it dribble down. He showed me how the water coursed over the corrugated metal to cool the milk; then I left, not wanting to be shown any sights which would stop me from drinking milk for the rest of my life.

I walked a little way down the road, under heavy trees, until I came to white park gates which I thought must belong to the Tichborne place. I wondered if the impostor had ever come down to drink and roister in the country, or whether he'd stayed in London the whole time, filling his 'mother's' house with boozy friends and gamblers, while she quietly backed him up and believed in him.

I could see no house, only lonely clumps of trees dotting the parkland. The heavy green loneliness filled me with melancholy. I turned back and decided to walk without stopping until I came to Winchester.

The nice warden lent me the money for my fare home and I caught a train that afternoon.

When I arrived at my grandfather's house I found my aunt and my cousin Margaret standing in the drive. Margaret (who had evidently come to stay for a few days) smiled at me, but my aunt gaped.

'I thought you were down in Devonshire,' she said.

'I was, but I ran out of money and had to get back quickly.'

My aunt's face clouded over; she looked worried and harrassed.

'We were just going out to tea. Will you come with us and sit in the car, or will you stay here?' she asked.

'Oh, I'll come with you and sit in the car, or go for a walk,' I decided hurriedly.

I realized that my aunt did not think me presentable for strangers, but when I learnt that we were going to see my elderly cousin May, who had been ill and was recuperating near Seaford, I wondered why I was to be made to sit in the car outside. She it was who had given me refuge when I came back to London after running away from school. She had been nice to me and I liked her.

'Can't I come in with you to see May?' I asked.

'No, you'll only upset her,' my aunt said. 'She doesn't expect to see you and it will be a shock to her.'

This was such a weak excuse that I could say no more. We drove on in silence until we came to the Downs above Seaford.

'You'd better drop me here,' I said with a certain amount of relish. 'May would never let me sit in the car outside her house, and she'd be bound to see me.'

My aunt stopped the car and I got out. Again she gave me an anxious, worried look.

'We'll pick you up here again at a quarter to six,' she said, looking at her watch.

The car started up, and I was left alone on the bare hillside. There was a little disused chalk quarry nearby; I climbed down between the miniature cliffs and sat down on a dusty ledge, sunning myself. My clothes were soon covered with white, and I began to sweat.

Sheltered from the wind, the sun seemed very hot. I took off my shirt, and the jagged chalk wall pricked and tickled when I lay back. A trickle of sweat ran into one of my eyes and stung; I heard the rush of a car on the road outside, then there was silence. I wondered if the time would ever pass until a quarter to six.

Somehow it did, for when at last I went out on to the road again, I saw a black beetle below me in the valley, which, as it came nearer, turned into my aunt's car.

She held open the door for me and said, 'I hope you haven't been bored up here.'

I tried not to make any direct answer. I felt aggrieved. In fact, I was sulking. My cousin squeezed my hand and smiled and said something in a low gay murmur to me, something like, 'It's too bad!' or 'Never mind!'

When we got back to the house my aunt asked:

'Well, and what are you going to do now?'

'If you'll give me some money I'll go off on my travels again,' I said. This sounded evil, like a blackmailing threat, I thought.

My aunt was talking as if, instead of saying that I would go away, I had said that I wanted to stay.

'It's too much for the maids with you as well as Margaret in the house, and – and I think it's such frightful cheek just to turn up like this without giving us any warning at all.' She had now become quite excited; the little stutter over the 'ands' had marked the change from normality.

'Of course I can't stay as you don't want to have me. But will you let me have some money? If not, I can't do anything. You can write to Daddy's office and get it back within the week,' I added as a rude afterthought.

My aunt went red and I went red. She hurried up to her bedroom, and I went up to Margaret's bedroom and sat on her bed with her for a few moments, looking at her drawings, and laughing and talking as naturally as I could.

My aunt came in with some pound notes and gave them to me. I thanked her and left the house without even going in to the drawing-room to see my grandfather.

Again I was setting out in the evening without knowing where I was to sleep. And again my feet led me to the river; but this time to a higher reach, to a place where the road-bridge had been washed away a hundred years ago. It had never been replaced, and now there was only a spindly black foot-bridge, high up on stilts above the water.

I walked over the tussocky field towards it, nursing my grievance and my loneliness. Loneliness pierced into me here; everything was still as death, until the wind came to bend the grass or stroke the leaves of the trees the wrong way. But when the gust stopped and the blades and the leaves fell back into place, the stillness seemed more binding than before.

Before the bridge was a place where boys would bathe; the banks had fallen in, making a wider pool. I sat down near the crumbling edge, where bare feet had smoothed and flattened the mud.

Looking across the water I wondered what to do. I had no plan, no looking-forward feeling. I was dead inside, with no adventurousness.

I threw a crumb of earth into the water, and as I watched the silky rings and folds spreading over the water I became conscious of another movement, above this one, on the other bank of the river. Someone was opening the garden gate of the old plastered farm-house, the only building in sight.

The figure was lichen-coloured, like the stone-slab roof of the house. Although he was quite near, his outline melted into the trees and the bushes. As he crossed the spidery black bridge and I saw him against the sky, I realized that he was young. From the lichen-colour of his clothes I had expected him to be old. He came swinging towards me over the uneven ground, putting his feet down in the loose, almost swaggering way which told me that he walked all day over rough fields and ploughed land.

'You going in?' he asked pleasantly, unrolling the dirty white towel which had been tucked under his arm.

For some reason I only smiled and shook my head. I think I must have been too surprised to speak, for, from his shining brass hair to his dung-caked boots, this was a very beautiful man. He seemed to have a liquid or varnish of life spread over his skin, his teeth, his eyes, his hair.

'If there are any women round here they're going to get an eyeful,' he said, and started to pull his shirt over his head. He undid his belt, and his breeches concertinaed into folds round his knees. He stood there with his head and arms enveloped in the shirt, and his legs entangled in the breeches. I heard his laughing and swearing, muffled by the shirt – he seemed to be trying to undo a button with his teeth – but I did not help him. I sat looking at his body, shocked by its junket whiteness. His arms and his face had been brick-dust colour, the skin taut and shining. I could hardly believe that the rest of his body was as white and matt as oatmeal. I knew that when he pulled his head and his arms out of the shirt he would look as if he wore long tawny gloves and helmet.

He sat down on the ground, unlaced his boots and peeled off his sweat-sticky socks, and the breeches which were exactly the colour of the mud and the cow-dung caked on them. The image jumped into my mind of myself as a small boy peeling a stick. It was the same – the scabby, silvery bark peeled off, leaving the living whiteness unprotected.

The man stood up, shook back his hair, and dived into the water. He came up spitting and laughing.

'Fucking filthy water!' he yelled. 'Fucking filthy, but it feels fine. You ought to come in.'

I shook my head again and went on staring at him. He stood up near the bank, so that the water gartered the middle of his calves, making him look like a broken statue in the bowl of a fountain. He disappeared again under the brown water.

He went on floundering, splashing, spitting, cursing, laughing until at last he crawled up the bank and lay down beside me with his eyes shut. I watched the water coursing off his body; the main stream flowed down his chest, over the mushroom-smooth belly, and lost itself at last in curly gold hair. I could just see the quicksilver drops fastening round single hairs, or weaving painfully through the golden bush. He glittered all over with these drops clinging to hair-points.

He opened his eyes, sat up, and started to rub his chest and arms roughly with the dirty towel. Red tingling lines and scribbles appeared on his skin.

'I'm down here working on the farm,' he volunteered abruptly.

I felt that I had to tell him what I did, in return.

'Oh, my sister's a very clever artist too,' he said. 'She's won scholarships and all sorts of things, and now she's going abroad. She's the pet lamb and I'm the black sheep,' he added with a rather too devilish grin.

How he interested me! I wanted him to go on talking until I knew his whole story. I waited, not asking any questions, afraid to show too much eagerness.

Gradually, in sharp jerky sentences, mixed with bravado laughing, he told me that he had no more to do with his family. They had given him up, and he had given them up. They didn't even know where he was. He earned his living as a farm-labourer.

'I like it, and one day I'll have a farm of my own,' he said.

It was delightful for me to be with someone who was in disgrace with his family; I warmed to him more and more. I wanted to tell him all about my aunt's cold welcome, but it sounded so tame after his daring story that I only allowed myself to hint that I too was not in high favour at home.

'I get tight most evenings, when I've got any money,' he said suddenly. 'There's nothing else to do. That was one of the troubles at home – they hated me boozing in the village pub. They said it was low.'

He went on to tell me of fights and brawls. Once on Christmas Day he had been locked up for fighting in the village street, outside the pub, when it closed in the afternoon. Even as I listened to these exciting stories I wondered how much was exaggeration. It seemed wonderful to me that his beautiful white teeth had not been knocked down his throat a long time ago. And as I imagined this happening, I had a real pain; the sort of pain that stabs at you when you see some beautifully made intricate thing threatened. I too, like his family, wished that he wouldn't booze so much. I wanted to ask him to be more sober, but of course did not dare to. Already, I felt, he must think me quite mild enough.

'And where are you going to sleep tonight?' he asked, looking at my rucksack.

'Oh, I don't know,' I said with special casualness. 'I just walked out as they didn't seem particularly pleased to see me. I only came back today from one long walking-tour. I've been right down to Devonshire,' I explained.

'I'd like to do that,' he mused, looking far away. 'I'd like to go walking all over Europe. I could earn a bit as I went along. They wouldn't give me anything!' he spat out at the end.

I waited a moment, then blurted out, 'Couldn't we do that together then? I think I could get a little money, and as you say, we could earn some more.'

If he had not taken me seriously I should have felt humiliated, but when he did take me seriously I saw immediately how badly matched we were. I saw us sulking or quarrelling as we trudged along a dusty white road in France or climbed a mountain in Austria. I would always fall below his bold bad standards; we would never understand each other. Yet, oh, how I wanted this adventure!

'I say, do you really think we could do that?' he asked, his eyes lighting up. 'It would have to be later in the year though. I've got to work here till the autumn.'

'That'll be just when I have to go back to the school,' I said.

I started to demolish the whole idea, except as an idea. I felt cowardly for not making it happen in some way; more than anything else at that moment I wanted to go on the journey with him, yet I still went on talking vaguely.

'It would be nice sometime,' I said.

He pulled on his clothes, then stood up, buckling on his belt. He held out his hand and I grasped it, getting a shock when I felt the horny palm, hard and brittle as celluloid.

'Good-bye,' we said, not even asking for each other's names or addresses.

I watched him the whole way. The legs, the shoulders and the towel swung in rhythm till he reached the garden gate. He turned and waved. I waved back and then started to run over the tussocks. I let the rucksack bang viciously on my back, and when I turned my ankle I was pleased at the pain. It made me feel less unbearably angry and frustrated.

I walked and ran until I had reached the deserted little railway station. There I boarded the first train to come in. It took me to Horsham where I had to wait for several hours.

When at last I got a train to Winchester I sat back and listened to the drumming of the wheels. There was no one to talk to; the other passengers looked ugly and they were half asleep.

But it ought to be exciting to travel at midnight, I thought. I ought to have adventures. Then I realized that I didn't want adventures, I wanted to be sleeping in a bedroom, with people that I liked near me. I felt sorry for myself, that I had to travel at midnight in a train to a strange town.

I seemed to be the only person awake in all Winchester. I had the midnight sense of power, the feeling of owning the streets I walked through to get to the city mill.

I knocked on the door and waited guiltily. There was no sound and I knocked again. It was now two o'clock; I heard it striking.

The warden came with her eyes bloated and thick with sleep. She had dragged on a curious khaki cotton dressing-gown which made her look like a rolled tobacco-pouch, and her short hair was sticking up in squalid spikes. She was furious.

'What the devil do you mean by coming at this time of night,' she said. 'I ought not to let you in.' But even as she spoke she held the door open and stood back for me to pass. She went on muttering for form's sake, but I knew it meant nothing.

'Cut along,' she said, 'and for Christ's sake don't wake the others up. If you do I hope they'll slay you.'

I stumbled through the whole length of the mill, not daring to put a light on. Draughts blew along the floors, up in the high barn ceiling, from window to window. Nothing fitted, there were chinks and cracks everywhere and pale light showing through them.

When I reached the men's dormitory I felt along the beds carefully, terrified of lying down on one already occupied.

Underneath, the water rushed. The noise covered everything; it even covered my thoughts and wiped them out. I lay down, satisfied to be here, not caring what I did tomorrow.

I paid back the money to the warden in the morning.

'Good at paying your debts, aren't you,' she said. 'That's one thing, but God I was annoyed when you got me up last night. It was two o'clock, you know. Two o'clock! You ought to be hung.' She laughed, and I apologized again.

On the wall in her little private room she had pinned a map of the Pilgrim's Way from Winchester to Canterbury.

'That's what I'll do,' I said, 'I'll walk along the Pilgrim's Way to Canterbury. Where can I get one of these little maps?'

She opened a drawer and gave me one.

'That'll be sixpence, sir,' she said, in a shopgirl's voice.

I took the little map, which was rather smudgy, being reproduced by that jelly process which makes use of a tray of jelly. I remembered seeing the tray of jelly when I first went to St Michael's. A master was printing songs for us to sing; and I watched, fascinated. The jelly, with the purplish stains of the writing on it, looked good to eat, but I knew it was poison.

The little map looked so simple; there was the Pilgrim's Way, clearly marked, all the way from Winchester to Canterbury. I said good-bye to the warden and started at once.

By that afternoon I was in difficulties; I had quite lost my way, and for some time had been walking across fields where no shadow of a path could be seen. Climbing fences and pushing through hedges had so exhausted and annoyed me that, when I finally came out on the edge of a huge ploughed field, I was ready to cry with rage. I started to swear aloud and snarl, and I felt real tears in my eyes. I sat down on the ground, resting my head on my knees. Little pictures of my childhood and stories about God floated about in my mind, and I felt better.

I stood up again, and then stepped on to the ploughed field; the pink-brown churned-up earth stuck to my shoes, until I was carrying two heavy balls on my feet. I ploughed on down the steep dip and up the other side. I swore not to stop until I reached grass again.

To feel the hardness again was wonderful. To know that the road led somewhere was wonderful too. I walked until I came to Four Marks, one of those country slums, all beaverboard and corrugated iron, which people seem to find so bright and cosy.

I knew there was a hostel nearby. I found the right bungalow and walked up to the front door. As I waited, I was surrounded and hemmed in by the heaviness of flower-smell and the vibrating of the bees. Rose leaves fell on other flowers, smothering them in white and pink. Everything was heavy, full and weighed-down.

The woman who came to the door seemed meagre in comparison. She had no juice. She looked at me too inquiringly.

'Yes?' she said.

'I've come for the night,' I answered, trying to make her smile.

She showed me to a room with beds in it and asked: 'What will you take for supper?'

'Oh, I'll make my own, thank you,' I said, 'I have food with me.'
The woman went away and I heard her talking to her husband. I started
to unpack the rye bread and honey and other nice things I had bought.

Both the man and the woman came back into the room and stood
over me.

'The other two gentlemen who've arrived are going to have our
supper,' the woman began.

'But I'd rather have my own food which I've bought. I don't want
meat,' I said.

'This isn't an ordinary hostel. We always make the meals,' she went
on stubbornly.

'Oh, I didn't know; you ought to put that in the little booklet. It
says there that every hostel has a place for cooking. But it doesn't
matter at all. I don't want to cook, I only want to eat my bread and
cheese and honey and chocolate.'

She shifted about on her feet and said again, 'This isn't an ordinary hostel.' But even as she said it, I knew that it *was* an ordinary
hostel and that she was only trying to blackmail me into eating her
offal so that she could make a little money out of my stay.

'I think I'll go on then,' I said as calmly as I could, 'I don't think
I'd really like to stay the night in an *extraordinary* hostel.'

'What do you mean – nothing *extraordinary* goes on here!'

I was delighted. I had touched the woman. She was anxiously pro-
tecting the decency of her house. I could not have done more if I'd
called it a bawdy house.

I said nothing, but packed up my honey and rye bread again. They
both watched me; the anxious look was still in their eyes. How
frightened they were of immorality! My silly words, said without
thought, had been charged with threat and evil meaning for them.

'Good-bye,' I said, going out of the door. They did not answer,
but stood staring after me, still looking dazed.

When I got into the road, I began to curse them. I had nowhere
to go for the night. I was tired. I was hungry.

When the bus slowed down in front of me, I ran, caught hold of
the chromium bar and pulled myself up.

'I want to go as far as I can,' I said to the conductor.

～

A man stopped and spoke to me as I sat in the field near Petersfield, eating my bread and honey and watching the sunset rage across the sky.

'That's a sight, ain't it!' he said, wrinkling the skin round his eyes and showing all his teeth in a wide grin.

'Yes, it's fine.'

'Over in a minute though,' he mused. He gave me another grin.

'Where are you going to spend the night then – under a haystack?' He seemed to find me very amusing; I had the impression that he was just able to keep back his chuckles.

'I shall go to the Youth Hostel at Harting, if I can find the way,' I said.

'It'll be dark before you get there,' he told me, still with the grin on his face. The sunset had turned his skin orange, and against this, the row of large white teeth were startling. A yellow cow's lick of hair curled round on his forehead. It was a nice fresh, clownish face.

'Why are you smiling at me?' I asked suddenly.

'Oh, I dunno, you look as if you was enjoying yourself, eating all that bread and honey out in the open.'

'I am,' I said.

I turned and looked straight into his eyes; they seemed to be bubbling over with exuberance, sparkling all along the edges with the beginning of laughter tears.

I caught some of his crazy gaiety, and grinned back; then we both laughed out aloud and became thoroughly friendly.

'I hope you'll find your way,' he said softly. He asked me more questions, still gazing at me. Even when he said good-night, he kept looking over his shoulder and waving his hand.

To be wished so much good was lovely. I got up and walked to Harting. And as I walked I remembered my relations and all the people who made me feel uncomfortable.

It's better to sleep in the ditch, I thought, than to thrust yourself on your relations.

Under the Downs are two ruined churches. They are ruined because in Victorian times the local grandee built a beautiful new church, large enough to serve the three parishes.

I climbed up to the ruins at Treyford, full of anger and rage. But perhaps they're better ruined than restored, I thought.

The walls were still standing all round me, but huge weeds and little trees pushed up through the floor, and the roof was off. I read the names on the tombstones and saw the church restored and converted into a house for me. I can never look at a ruin without converting it into a house for me. From the nearby farm I heard voices and the rattle of milk cans. I brushed through the nettles again, stinging my knees, and walked on.

At a turn in the lane I came on a house with all the windows open. There was a board up to say that a special sort of dog was bred there. A complaining woman's voice called out from upstairs, and I heard a man in the garden answering just not loud enough for her to hear. She called again, and I passed on down the lane.

Several years afterwards I was to meet some people who said, 'We used to breed dogs near Treyford.'

'Then I heard you calling to each other one summer afternoon,' I said. And I shall always remember them like that, the woman calling from the upstairs window and the man answering so that she would not hear.

When I reached Cocking, I found that the hostel was a wooden hut in the grounds of the vicarage. The vicar was giving a children's party in the large common-room, and I was immediately roped in to help. The vicar's niece of fifteen seized on me, sized me up shrewdly and told me to organize the tug-of-war. The children took me for the most tremendous joke, quite the funniest part of the evening. My face turned to deep crimson. I was helpless. They refused to play tug-of-war but gripped my arms, my legs, my waist, saying the most insolent, humiliating things as they swung on me lovingly.

The little niece came bustling up. 'Now children, leave Mr – Mr – leave Mister alone.' She finished hurriedly and with a threat in her voice, as she felt she had been made to look silly by not knowing my name.

The children fell away from me, knowing that, party or no party, she was quite capable of slapping them if they did not obey.

The tug-of-war was properly organized. The children screamed. The vicar came up to speak to me. He had food marks on his waistcoat and scurf on his collar and his round little eyes looked watery behind his glasses. His pink lips looked wet too. He was laughing and smiling and chortling, watching everything as if he'd paid for his seat at the theatre. He didn't seem to like or dislike anyone.

When the last child had left, and I was alone in the large wooden hut, I stood on a chair and looked at the books on a high shelf. They were old books. Perhaps some other parson had left them behind when he died. There was a squat line of Johnson's *Lives of the Poets*. The gold medallions on their spines still shone very bright, but the leather was tough and furry with age.

I took one down and began to read the biographical note, as I ate puffed rice and milk.

Afterwards I wandered through the vicarage shrubbery and came out on the road. I walked till I came to a pub. People were standing about in groups whispering, and then guffawing loudly. The door of the urinal rattled. Men were whistling inside and striking matches; I could see the momentary glow above the cream-washed wall. More laughter, a little singing, broken off as suddenly as it was started, and then, 'Good-night, Ted, Good-night, Bob,' name after name was called out ceremoniously.

I turned back, listening to the voices of the group just in front of me. They clung close together, with their arms round one another. They were not drunk. They seemed to be telling very elaborate dirty jokes, but all I could distinguish were the swear words. These jumped out and hung in the air like certain insistent notes in some piece of music which is being played too far away to be properly heard.

I sat with my back against the wall of Cocking Churchyard. The morning sun shone full on my face as I tried to make a picture of a gate, a field, a hillside and three posts. I had wanted to do it like this, with the sun behind, making everything rather flat and colourless and silvery.

I thought that what I was doing was good; it was really the best watercolour I had ever done. I was so pleased that I had the expensive paper with me. Now a little dry brush work for the hedge,

I thought; and I prayed that only the right amount of colour would come off my brush.

When I could do no more, I lay back and looked at my picture in admiration. For once I felt almost delighted. 'Is it only my mood, or is the picture much better?' I wondered. It's like the Paul Nash I saw when I was fourteen.